Artic Nightmare

Artic Nightmare

Magnum Tenebrosum

Darkness Studios

CONTENTS

CONTENTS

CONTENTS

Artic Nightmare

By

Magnum Tenebrosum

Foreword

by

Magnum Tenebrosum

In the shadowed corners of the cosmos, where the human mind dare not tread, lies the inspiration for this book. As a writer entrenched in the realm of horror, specifically Lovecraftian Cosmic Horror, I have always been drawn to the enigmatic, the unfathomable, and the terrifying unknown.

The genesis of "Arctic Nightmare" emerged from my relentless pursuit of the cosmic horrors that lie beyond our understanding, beyond the thin veil of sanity that separates us from the abyss. It is a descent into the depths of existential dread, a journey that beckons the reader to question their place in the grand cosmic scheme.

The narratives within this book serve as windows into the minds of those who have, often unwittingly, crossed paths with an entity whose malevolence defies comprehension. Each story is a testament to the fragility of human sanity, an exploration of obsession, and a confrontation with the ultimate insignificance of our species in the face of cosmic forces.

In the tradition of Lovecraft, I invite you to delve into the darkness, to peer into the abyss, and to embrace the unknown. "Arctic Nightmare" is an exploration of the terrors that lurk at the fringes of our understanding, and I hope it leaves you with a lingering sense of cosmic dread that will forever haunt your thoughts.

Magnum Tenebrosum

3

Prologue
The Forgotten Civilization
In the heart of the frozen wasteland that is Antarctica, a civilization long forgotten thrived in the perpetual darkness of the polar night. Their origins and history were shrouded in mystery, their existence known to only a few.

This civilization was comprised of highly evolved humanoid beings, their society steeped in enigmatic ceremonies and arcane rituals that defied human comprehension. Within the prologue, this ancient culture is vividly described, emphasizing the strangeness and eerie beauty of their underground world.

It was a realm hidden beneath layers of ice, a sprawling subterranean network of intricate tunnels and chambers that seemed to defy the harsh reality of the surface world. Here, they worshipped an outer god, a deity of unfathomable power, with rituals that transcended human notions of time and space.

The caverns were adorned with bizarre, hieroglyphic carvings, their meaning known only to the ancient civilization. Strange sculptures and altars stood as silent witnesses to the bizarre ceremonies conducted in the name of their otherworldly deity.

As they delved deeper into the bowels of the earth, their rituals grew darker and more incomprehensible. It was in these depths that they made contact with an entity, an intelligence that resided in the heart of Antarctica, trapped and waiting.

The civilization, believing that they could harness the entity's power, entered into a pact with it. They offered sacrifices and performed unspeakable rites to bind themselves to this entity. In return, the entity granted them knowledge and insight that extended far beyond the reach of human wisdom.

But power comes at a price. As their knowledge expanded, so did their hubris. The rituals grew more extreme, their society teetering on the precipice of madness. The entity, patient and malevolent, watched as the civilization spiraled into a cosmic nightmare.

It was this civilization's downfall that set in motion a series of events that would cast a shadow over the ages to come, leaving the entity trapped and waiting for a new vessel, a new conduit to bring its darkness into the world once more.

The leaders of this civilization entered into unholy pacts with an entity that transcended the boundaries of time and space. This entity, known only as "The Whisperer in Ice," was believed to be an emissary of the Elder Gods, an entity of unimaginable power and cosmic significance.

Through these pacts, the leaders of the civilization gained access to forbidden knowledge and supernatural abilities. They sought to tap into the very heart of the cosmos, to grasp the secrets of the universe that had eluded all of humanity's endeavors. It was an offer too tempting to resist, for the allure of such cosmic enlightenment was powerful beyond measure.

The entity, the Whisperer in Ice, whispered secrets in the dead of night, revealing knowledge that defied the laws of nature and reason. The leaders of the civilization, in their ambition and desperation, believed that they could reshape the world, bend reality to their will, and ascend to godhood.

Yet, the price they paid was not a mere pact but a descent into madness. As their minds expanded to comprehend the incomprehensible, so too did their souls become tainted by the malevolent essence of the entity. Its influence began to seep into every aspect of their lives, subtly corrupting their thoughts, their actions, and their very essence.

The entity's whispers grew louder, more insistent, and more maddening. It promised them power and knowledge, but it exacted a toll that left them spiritually and morally bankrupt. They found themselves trapped in a web of obsession, paranoia, and cosmic horror. Their society crumbled, and the once-thriving civilization became a nightmarish labyrinth of despair.

The years passed, and as the civilization basked in the newfound knowledge and power granted by the entity, they descended into a state of decadence. Their once-pure intentions were tainted by the entity's malevolence, and their society crumbled under the weight of their own hubris.

Once a beacon of enlightenment and scientific pursuit, their civilization now stood as a stark testament to their decline. The intellectual and artistic endeavors that had once flourished in their underground realm were now nothing more than relics of a bygone era.

Individuals who had once been brilliant scientists, visionary artists, and wise leaders became mere vessels for the entity's will. The entity's influence had transformed them into hollow shells, obsessed with serving its inscrutable desires. Their thoughts and actions were no longer their own, as they blindly obeyed the entity's nightmarish commands.

The underground realm, once a hub of intellectual exploration and artistic expression, had turned into a desolate and sinister place. The intricate tunnels and chambers, once filled with the echoes of debate and creativity, now lay in eerie silence, their walls bearing witness to the corruption that had befallen the civilization.

The entity's whispers echoed through the caverns, filling the minds of those who remained with unspeakable dread. It reveled in their decadence, for it knew that their fall from grace was inevitable. The once-thriving culture had become a haunting reminder of the horrors that lurked beneath the surface, waiting for the right moment to rise once more.

As the civilization's downfall was sealed in a maelstrom of decadence and malevolence, the prologue takes a final, chilling glimpse into the cosmic forces represented by the entity. Its inscrutable desires and its connection to the outer gods hinted at a power beyond human comprehension.

The narrative transitions to the present day, where a new group, unaware of the horrors hidden beneath the ice, stands at the brink of destiny. These individuals, driven by curiosity and scientific pursuit, are about to cross paths with the very entity that once ensnared the ancient civilization. They are about to awaken forces that should have remained dormant in the icy depths.

Chapter 1

The Specialist in Antarctic Studies

In the frigid heart of the Antarctic, where the howling winds and relentless blizzards obscure the line between reality and nightmare, Dr. Evelyn Winters emerged as a beacon of unwavering dedication and unparalleled expertise.

Evelyn, the story's protagonist, was a seasoned expert in the field of Antarctic studies. Her academic and professional background was nothing short of remarkable, a testament to her relentless pursuit of knowledge. Years of tireless exploration and research had honed her into a scholar of the highest order.

Evelyn's journey into the depths of the frozen wilderness began long ago, driven by an insatiable curiosity and a determination to unravel the enigmas concealed by the ice. Her scholarly pursuits had led her through the intricate labyrinths of Antarctic history and the unique ecosystems that thrived in this unforgiving realm.

She was a dedicated scientist, her passion fueled by an unyielding commitment to uncovering the secrets hidden beneath the ice. The harsh conditions, the isolation, and the omnipresent cold were mere challenges to be conquered on her path to enlightenment. Her knowledge of the Antarctic landscape and its mysteries was second to none.

Evelyn's reputation extended beyond the academic world. She was known not only for her extensive research but also for her fearlessness in the face of adversity. She had weathered the harshest blizzards, crossed treacherous ice fields, and delved into the very depths of the Antarctic abyss, all in pursuit of truth.

As a specialist in Antarctic studies, Dr. Evelyn Winters stood at the precipice of a journey that would push her to the limits of her knowledge and courage. Her unquenchable thirst for understanding would lead her to confront ancient horrors that lurked beneath the ice, and her academic prowess would be tested as never before. In the depths of the frozen nightmare, she was about to embark on an expedition that would challenge the very essence of her being.

Dr. Winters' life took an unexpected turn on a particularly bitter Antarctic morning. The chill in the air seemed to carry a sense of foreboding, but as she entered her research station, she couldn't have foreseen the enigmatic invitation that awaited her.

The message was cryptic, its origins unknown. It was an invitation to join a select scientific expedition team, one that hinted at the opportunity of a lifetime, a venture that could redefine her career and reshape her understanding of Antarctica. The very mention of the expedition sent a shiver down her spine, one that wasn't caused by the icy winds outside.

The intrigue of the invitation and the mystery shrouding the upcoming adventure ignited a fire of curiosity within Evelyn. It was an alluring proposition, a journey into the unknown that beckoned her to push the boundaries of her knowledge and experience. Her heart raced with the possibilities, and her mind was consumed by the enigma of it all.

As she stood at the precipice of this decision, Dr. Evelyn Winters faced a choice that would alter the course of her life. She could stay within the familiar boundaries of her academic pursuits, a life of rigorous research and academic solitude. Or, she could embark on an adventure that held the promise of discovery beyond imagination, even if it meant venturing into the very heart of an Arctic nightmare.

Dr. Winters' decision set her on a course that led to an isolated research facility in the heart of Antarctica. The journey was arduous, and the facility lay hidden amidst the unforgiving ice and snow, far removed from the reaches of civilization. The very remoteness of this place was a testament to its seclusion, accentuating the sense of isolation and vulnerability that would come to define her experience.

As she arrived at the facility, the stark and foreboding landscape unfolded before her. The immense, icy tundra stretched as far as the eye could see, a desolate and unforgiving expanse. The research station, a solitary beacon of human presence in this polar wilderness, stood as a refuge from the unrelenting cold, but it was also a reminder of the harsh realities of life in this unforgiving realm.

The extreme conditions of the Antarctic served as a constant reminder of the treacherous journey Dr. Winters had embarked upon. The biting cold, the perpetual darkness, and the howling winds painted a stark contrast to the warmth and comfort of her previous life. In the midst of this frozen abyss, she found herself on the threshold of a chilling adventure, where the secrets of the past and the horrors that awaited beneath the ice would challenge her in ways she could never have imagined.

The wind howled through the frozen wilderness of Antarctica, carrying with it the secrets of a land forgotten by time. Dr. Evelyn Winters stood at the edge of this desolate expanse, her breath visible in the frigid air. The weight of expectations bore down on her as she gazed at the isolated research facility in the distance, nestled amidst the unrelenting ice and snow.

Evelyn's reputation as an expert in Antarctic studies had brought her to this point. Years of tireless exploration and research had culminated in this moment, an invitation that hinted at an adventure of a lifetime. The intrigue of the unknown, the mysteries hidden beneath the ice, and the enigmatic circumstances surrounding the invitation had ignited a fire of curiosity within her.

As she made her way towards the research facility, the stark landscape served as a constant reminder of the challenges that lay ahead. The isolation, the extreme conditions, and the relentless cold were all part of the harsh realities of life in the polar wilderness. But Evelyn was not deterred; she was driven by a thirst for knowledge that knew no bounds.

The anticipation of the discoveries to come, as well as the uncertainty of what awaited her in the icy depths, were palpable. Her journey was about to begin, and she was keenly aware of the pivotal role she was destined to play in the unfolding narrative. The ancient horrors of Antarctica and the pursuit of enlightenment were on a collision course, and Dr. Evelyn Winters stood at the epicenter of this impending clash, ready to confront the mysteries that lay beneath the ice and the nightmares that lurked in the polar darkness.

5

Chapter 2

The Journey to the Remote Outpost

The journey to the remote research facility in the heart of Antarctica was a perilous odyssey that Dr. Evelyn Winters and the scientific expedition team were determined to undertake. This diverse team of experts, each possessing unique skills in various fields, was united by a shared sense of purpose, bound by a mission that transcended the boundaries of ordinary scientific exploration.

As they embarked on this formidable journey, the team recognized the immense challenges that lay before them. Navigating treacherous terrain, enduring the biting cold, and facing the unpredictable whims of the Antarctic wilderness were all part of the trials they would confront. But their resolute determination was their driving force, an unwavering commitment to delve deeper into the icy wilderness and unearth the enigmas concealed within.

The experts in the expedition team had been carefully selected for their roles, each bringing their own expertise to the mission. From geologists to biologists, meteorologists to historians, they were a collective force of knowledge, prepared to confront the unknown. Their journey into the heart of the Antarctic abyss was an expedition into the depths of the human spirit, a testament to the unyielding pursuit of discovery.

As they pressed forward into the frozen unknown, the facility stood as a distant beacon of hope, an outpost of human presence in this desolate realm. The isolation of the facility and the formidable challenges they faced on their journey only served to intensify the sense of anticipation and trepidation that gripped the team. The secrets hidden beneath the ice, the enigmatic entity lurking in the subterranean depths, and the cosmic horrors that awaited were yet to reveal themselves, but this journey was the first step into the heart of the Arctic nightmare.

As the expedition team arrived at the remote research facility, the profound isolation of the Antarctic landscape enveloped them. The facility, a testament to human resilience and scientific ambition, stood in stark contrast to the vast, unending snow and ice that stretched to the horizon in every direction.

The unforgiving environment of Antarctica was nothing short of awe-inspiring, yet equally treacherous. The biting cold, the blinding whiteness, and the relentless winds were all vividly described, emphasizing the harshness of the Antarctic wilderness. It was a realm of extremes, where the human spirit was tested against the forces of nature, and where the fine line between survival and peril was as thin as the ice beneath their feet.

The isolation of the facility became even more pronounced as the team settled in. Surrounded by the desolation of the polar landscape, they were cut off from the outside world. Communication with their home base, already tenuous, became increasingly limited. The sense of being marooned in an icy wasteland was inescapable, and the facility itself began to take on an eerie, isolated aura.

As the team acclimated to their new surroundings, the weight of their endeavor became increasingly apparent. The mysteries that awaited them, the ancient horrors hidden beneath the ice, and the entity that had long slumbered in the subterranean depths were about to reveal themselves. The facility, a refuge and a prison in equal measure, would be their home in the heart of the Arctic nightmare, where the boundaries between exploration and terror would blur with each passing day.

The research facility had been strategically placed near the entrance to the subterranean cave system where the ancient civilization once worshipped the outer god. Dr. Evelyn Winters and the rest of the team were keenly aware of the historical significance of this location, which held the potential to unveil long-buried secrets, but also concealed untold horrors.

Their arrival at the facility marked the beginning of their arduous journey into the unknown. The team had been meticulously prepared for this endeavor, armed with knowledge and equipment to delve into the subterranean depths. The anticipation of what they might discover in this enigmatic place hung heavy in the air, a mixture of excitement and foreboding that coursed through their veins.

The subterranean caves, shrouded in darkness and mystery, were both a gateway to enlightenment and a portal to the abyss. The echoes of the past, the rituals of the ancient civilization, and the entity that had long remained dormant within these depths beckoned them further. Their torches illuminated the passage into the unknown, casting eerie shadows on the cave walls.

With each step they took, they ventured closer to the heart of the Arctic nightmare. The facility, the subterranean labyrinth, and the frigid wilderness that surrounded them were the stage for a story that had been hidden beneath the ice for millennia. Dr. Winters and her team were now poised on the precipice of discovery, ready to face the secrets and horrors that lay in wait within the subterranean depths.

The initial days at the research facility were marked by a growing sense of unease among the expedition team. Despite the camaraderie that had developed among the scientists, the facility's isolation and the unsettling history of the subterranean cave system cast a shadow of foreboding over their new home.

The vast, frozen wilderness outside seemed to press in on them, the endless expanse of snow and ice a reminder of their profound isolation. The weight of history, of the ancient civilization's rituals and pacts with an otherworldly entity, hung heavy in the air. It was as though the very walls of the facility bore witness to the secrets buried beneath the ice.

Amid the complex machinery and scientific instruments that filled the facility, the team members couldn't help but feel like intruders in a place that had long been abandoned by humanity. The foreboding atmosphere was punctuated by the occasional creak of the structure, the howling of the wind, and the echoes of their footsteps in the cold corridors.

The arrival at the facility had set the stage for the exploration and investigation that would follow. Their fate had become inexorably entwined with the ancient horrors lurking beneath the ice, and the shadow of the unknown loomed large over their every move. Dr. Evelyn Winters and her team were now poised on the precipice of a journey that would test the limits of their knowledge, their courage, and their very humanity as they delved deeper into the heart of the Arctic nightmare.

Chapter 3

The Descent into Darkness

With an unquenchable thirst for knowledge and an unwavering resolve, Dr. Evelyn Winters and the scientific expedition team embarked on a treacherous expedition into the subterranean caves hidden beneath the Antarctic ice. These underground passages, concealed from the world for untold ages, formed an enigmatic maze that wound its way into the very heart of the frozen continent.

The descent into darkness was a journey fraught with both anticipation and apprehension. The team's determination to uncover the secrets hidden within the subterranean labyrinth was palpable as they descended deeper into the frigid depths. The beams of their headlamps, like miniature suns in the oppressive darkness, created eerie, dancing patterns on the icy walls that surrounded them.

The cave system, a world of shadows and secrets, was a place where the past and the present intersected. The ancient rituals of the vanished civilization still resonated within the subterranean chambers, echoing through time. The team members could almost feel the weight of history pressing down on them as they ventured further into the enigmatic depths, the air growing colder and the silence more oppressive with each step.

As they delved deeper into the labyrinth, the boundaries between reality and myth began to blur. The frozen passageways seemed to breathe with an ancient, eldritch presence, and the team's courage was tested as they encountered strange, unexplained phenomena. Dr.

Winters and her team were now immersed in the heart of the Arctic nightmare, where the distinction between exploration and terror had become increasingly indistinct.

As Dr. Evelyn Winters and her scientific expedition team pressed further into the subterranean depths, they remained oblivious to the fact that their presence and exploration were awakening an ancient entity. This was the same consciousness that had slumbered for millennia beneath the Antarctic ice, hidden from the world's knowledge. As they ventured deeper into the labyrinthine caves, subtle disturbances and inexplicable phenomena began to manifest, signaling the entity's slow emergence from its eons-old prison.

The entity, a malevolent force that had long been forgotten by humanity, stirred from its ageless slumber. These disturbances within the caves took on eerie and uncanny forms. Strange, echoing whispers reverberated through the subterranean passages, as if the very walls themselves were attempting to communicate. Shadows moved of their own volition, casting disturbing silhouettes on the icy walls. The temperature dropped suddenly and precipitously, leaving a chill in the bones of the explorers.

Unbeknownst to the team, the entity's awareness grew with each passing moment. It had long waited for an opportunity to reassert itself in the world, and now, with intruders in its ancient domain, it began to take notice. It watched, waited, and plotted its return to a world it had once known, a world where it had wielded unimaginable power.

The disturbance within the caves was but a prelude to the malevolent force's impending awakening, and it would not remain dormant for much longer. Dr. Evelyn Winters and her team were on the precipice of a discovery that would change the course of their lives and uncover an ancient terror hidden beneath the ice of Antarctica.

Deeper into the subterranean maze they ventured, and with each step, an unsettling sensation of being watched and followed clung to the expedition team. It was as if unseen eyes observed their every move, their very presence stirring the ancient forces that had long slumbered in the heart of the Antarctic ice. Shadows, cast by the flickering beams of their headlamps, seemed to take on a life of their own, dancing in grotesque patterns on the icy walls.

Whispers, not quite human, reverberated through the narrow passages, carrying cryptic messages that evaded comprehension. The voices, ethereal and indistinct, teased at the edges of the explorers' awareness, sowing the seeds of disquiet and doubt. It was a chorus of the long-forgotten, the murmurs of an entity that had transcended the boundaries of time and space.

The narrative itself seemed to take on an ominous hue, becoming increasingly permeated with a sense of unease and foreboding. The team's vulnerability in the heart of the subterranean labyrinth was now painfully evident, as they navigated the intricate, icy passages that led deeper into the bowels of the earth.

Dr. Evelyn Winters and her team were adrift in a world where the line between reality and the supernatural blurred, where their every step took them further into the clutches of a malevolent entity that had long awaited its return to the realm of the living. They had entered a nightmarish realm where the ancient and the modern converged, and the boundaries of reality were stretched to their limits.

The expedition's relentless exploration began to yield its first hints of a long-lost civilization, as artifacts and enigmatic markings within the cave system were revealed. These discoveries shed a feeble light on the history of the civilization that had once fervently worshipped the outer god, an entity of cosmic significance and otherworldly power.

Dr. Evelyn Winters and her team meticulously documented their findings, unearthing relics that hinted at rituals and practices that defied human understanding. The enigmatic markings, etched into the icy walls, spoke of a culture steeped in esoteric knowledge and spiritual devotion to the entity known as "The Whisperer in Ice." It was a history that, until now, had remained hidden in the shadows of time.

With each artifact and cryptic symbol they uncovered, the tension among the expedition team grew. The very air in the cave seemed to vibrate with the weight of cosmic horrors long concealed beneath the ice. The narrative now stood on the precipice of revealing the chilling truths that awaited discovery. Dr. Winters and her team, driven by an insatiable curiosity, were about to unearth secrets that had been buried for millennia, and their quest for knowledge would bring them face to face with the eldritch forces lurking in the heart of the Antarctic nightmare.

Chapter 4

The Whisperer's Influence

In the heart of the subterranean labyrinth, where the very walls seemed to pulse with the weight of untold secrets, the ancient entity known as the Whisperer in Ice seized an opportunity to manifest its malevolent presence once more. As the expedition team delved deeper into the caves, the entity's consciousness began to stir, and it cast its sinister gaze upon the unsuspecting scientists.

Its choice of vessel was subtle and cunning, as one of the scientists unwittingly became the conduit for the entity's dark will. The entity's takeover was depicted as a gradual and insidious process. It crept into the scientist's mind like a shadow, slowly gaining control over their thoughts and actions.

The possessed scientist began to experience disorienting visions and eerie whispers that seemed to emanate from the very walls of the cave. These visions, a blend of haunting memories from the ancient civilization and glimpses of a cosmic reality beyond human comprehension, disoriented the scientist and eroded their grip on reality.

Dr. Evelyn Winters and the rest of the team were initially unaware of the encroaching darkness that now dwelled within their midst. The entity's malevolent influence began to take root, setting in motion a series of events that would test the limits of the team's sanity and challenge their understanding of reality itself. The expedition, once driven by the pursuit of knowledge, had now become a descent into the depths of cosmic horror, where the boundaries between the seen and the unseen grew increasingly blurred.

As the days passed within the subterranean darkness, the scientist who had unwittingly become the host for the entity began to exhibit alarming symptoms. These signs, initially perceived as mere maladies, painted a sinister picture of an unseen affliction.

The possessed scientist's condition manifested as an escalating fever, causing their body to burn with an unnatural heat. Shivers wracked their frame, yet it was not the chill of the Antarctic caves that gripped them. It was an unshakable sense of dread, a foreboding that whispered of ancient horrors lurking in the shadows.

Within the research facility, the emergence of these symptoms triggered a growing concern among the team. The expedition members, once a close-knit group bound by shared purpose, now found themselves cast into an abyss of fear and paranoia. Whispers of contagion filled the icy corridors, and the true source of the affliction remained hidden, veiled in mystery. The suspense reached its zenith as the expedition team grappled with the unknown, unaware that an insidious entity had taken residence among them, weaving its dark influence into the very fabric of their reality.

Deep within the heart of the subterranean labyrinth, the entity's insidious influence grew stronger. Unbeknownst to the expedition team, the entity seized control of the possessed scientist's actions, like a puppeteer pulling strings in the shadows.

Under the entity's malevolent guidance, the possessed scientist tampered with equipment and artifacts hidden within the cave. They were drawn to symbols and relics that had long been untouched, their actions guided by a force beyond their understanding. The entity's manipulations extended into the very heart of the ancient civilization's secrets, unraveling the threads of knowledge that had been sealed away for eons.

As the entity's actions became increasingly malevolent, the possessed scientist's behavior grew erratic and unpredictable. They exhibited a sinister determination that was at odds with their former self, leading the expedition team into uncharted territories within the caves. It was here, in the depths of the subterranean realm, that the true extent of the entity's power to manipulate and control became evident.

The team, unaware of the malevolent force that had taken root among them, found themselves at the mercy of an entity that could bend the will of its host to its dark desires. The growing danger posed by the entity's presence, its ability to manipulate, and the team's vulnerability to its influence set the stage for a harrowing descent into the heart of cosmic horror, where the line between reality and nightmare blurred with each passing moment.

With each passing day, the possessed scientist's condition deteriorated, their grip on reality slipping further. Yet amid their affliction, they began to utter cryptic hints, alluding to an unseen intelligence that guided their actions. Their words were laced with the unsettling suggestion that something far more sinister than a common infection had taken root.

These cryptic hints did not go unnoticed among the team. Suspicion and unease swept through the research facility like a chilling draft, and the expedition members found themselves confronted with a disturbing realization. The possessed scientist's words, spoken in riddles and whispers, painted a haunting picture of an entity beyond human comprehension.

The team, still grappling with the profound mysteries of the subterranean caves and the inexplicable affliction that had befallen them, remained in the dark about the true nature of the entity. As the horrors lurking beneath the Antarctic ice continued to unfurl, the expedition members were drawn further into the depths of the unknown, their perceptions of reality forever altered by the malevolent force that had been awakened in their midst.

Chapter 5

The Deterioration of the Possessed Scientist

As days turned into haunting nights within the research facility, the scientist who had fallen under the entity's ominous influence bore the brunt of an inexorable descent into darkness. Their physical condition worsened with alarming speed, and their mental state began to unravel, thread by fragile thread.

The possessed scientist's behaviors grew increasingly bizarre and disturbing, an unsettling transformation that could not be concealed from their fellow team members. Their eyes, once filled with the spark of curiosity, had grown hollow, and their once-rational thoughts had devolved into a maddening frenzy. They had become a vessel for the entity's malevolence, and as the days passed, their connection to reality dissolved like ice in the relentless Antarctic wind.

The narrative painted a vivid and chilling portrait of the possessed scientist's harrowing experience. It was a journey into the depths of madness, where the boundaries of sanity blurred, and the line between the real and the surreal became indistinguishable. The expedition members watched in terror as a once-cherished colleague succumbed to an unseen malevolence, their fear intensifying with each passing moment.

The possessed scientist's transformation did not occur in isolation; it unfolded within the scrutinizing gaze of their fellow team members. As the days wore on, the team's collective unease began to manifest in whispered conversations and exchanged glances laden with suspicion. The changes in the possessed scientist's demeanor had not gone unnoticed, and a creeping sense of alarm gripped the isolated research facility.

In hushed tones and furtive discussions, the team members shared their growing concerns about the possessed scientist's increasingly erratic behavior. They questioned the inexplicable actions and cryptic remarks that had become a hallmark of the scientist's daily life. Each unexplained incident, each disturbance that defied reason, added another layer of dread to the already tense atmosphere within the facility.

The mounting tension within the group created a palpable sense of disquiet, as they grappled with the realization that they were confronting something beyond the realm of scientific understanding. The line between reality and nightmare had blurred, and the once-unbreakable trust among the team members had begun to erode in the face of the insidious presence that had infiltrated their lives.

Fueled by a potent cocktail of paranoia and fear, the team arrived at a grim and unsettling decision that seemed to offer the only semblance of security within their frigid, isolated confines. The creeping doubts and the haunting uncertainty had grown to such an extent that the team felt compelled to take drastic measures. They decided, with a heavy heart, to isolate themselves within the research facility.

The choice to quarantine themselves was a stark reflection of the mounting tension and the profound desperation that had begun to consume them. It was as if the pervasive dread had woven a chilling web around their collective consciousness, pushing them to take extreme actions in a bid to safeguard their own lives.

As the isolation measures were put into place, the narrative underscored the profound alienation that gripped the team. Their interactions became strained, their voices seldom rose above a whisper, and the research facility, once a symbol of scientific endeavor, transformed into a cold and desolate prison. It was in this atmosphere of dread and suspicion that the entity's insidious influence continued to fester, unseen and unforgiving.

The decision to isolate themselves within the research facility was not one taken lightly, and it cast a long, chilling shadow over their already strained psyches. The isolation, meant to protect them from an unseen and malevolent force, gave rise to an intense exploration of the team members' psychological struggles.

Each day, as the Antarctic night raged outside, the weight of their predicament pressed down on them like a suffocating shroud. The unknown nature of the entity that had possessed their colleague, the deteriorating condition of the unfortunate scientist, and the unsettling events within the facility all combined to create a pervasive sense of dread that hung in the air like an invisible specter.

Within the confines of the facility, the team members were locked in a psychological battle, not only against the entity but also against their own fear. They wrestled with the terrifying uncertainty of what lay ahead, unaware that the true source of their terror was, in fact, lurking within their midst, an ancient evil waiting patiently for its moment to strike.

As the cold darkness of the Antarctic night enveloped the research facility, the narrative emphasized the lingering dread that clung to the team like a second skin, setting the stage for the harrowing trials that lay ahead in their battle for survival.

9

Chapter 6
The Specialist's Initiative
In the midst of the growing isolation and the ominous dread that gripped the research facility, Dr. Evelyn Winters emerged as a guiding light in the darkness. Her extensive background in Antarctic studies, combined with a profound dedication to her work and her colleagues, propelled her into a pivotal role within the isolated facility.

Dr. Winters' unwavering commitment to uncovering the truth and her deep sense of responsibility for the safety of her team were the driving forces behind her decision to take the lead. She understood that the situation was dire, and that something beyond their comprehension had taken hold of one of their own.

Her role as a specialist in Antarctic studies was not limited to her academic prowess; it extended to her ability to navigate the treacherous waters of fear and uncertainty. She became a source of inspiration and a beacon of hope for the team members who, in their darkest hours, looked to her for guidance and support.

With resolute determination, Dr. Winters embarked on an investigation to understand the cause of the perceived infection and the deteriorating condition of the possessed scientist. Her expertise and her unwavering commitment to protecting her team propelled her into a leadership position, setting the stage for a relentless quest for answers within the frigid, isolated confines of the research facility.

Dr. Winters' relentless investigation into the inexplicable events transpiring within the research facility led her down a path of discovery that defied all scientific explanation. As she delved deeper into the mystery, she began to unveil the true nature of the entity that lurked within their midst.

It was through cryptic messages, eerie behaviors exhibited by the possessed scientist, and an ever-growing sense of unease that Dr. Winters started to decipher the enigma that was the entity. The entity's presence, which had remained hidden in the shadows, began to manifest itself more openly, albeit in subtle and disturbing ways.

These revelations were the turning point in Dr. Winters' understanding of their predicament. She realized that they were not dealing with a mere scientific anomaly or a conventional threat. Instead, they faced a force that transcended the boundaries of human comprehension—a malevolent entity that had lain dormant for ages and was now reasserting its dominance.

Dr. Winters' expertise and unwavering courage were both her greatest assets and her Achilles' heel. While her knowledge of the Antarctic terrain and her tenacity were invaluable in her quest for answers, they also made her acutely aware of the cosmic horrors they were entangled with, a knowledge that cast a chilling shadow over her every move.

The entity, having chosen Dr. Winters as the focal point of its interactions, embarked on a sinister campaign of manipulation. It played upon her curiosity, leading her down a shadowy path of enigmatic communication and disturbing visions.

Through cryptic messages and unsettling images, the entity wove a tapestry of confusion and dread in Dr. Winters' mind. It spoke in riddles, offering glimpses of knowledge that seemed just out of reach. Visions of otherworldly landscapes and grotesque beings blurred the lines between reality and nightmare, leaving Dr. Winters to question her own sanity.

These manipulations deepened the cosmic horror that enveloped the research facility. Dr. Winters found herself caught in a web of the entity's making, struggling to discern its true intentions and the extent of its otherworldly powers. As the narrative unfolded, the entity's malevolent presence cast an ever-lengthening shadow over their desperate struggle for survival.

Dr. Winters' shoulders bore the heavy burden of responsibility as she assumed the role of guiding the team through their harrowing ordeal. Her leadership was not merely a matter of choice but a profound sense of duty, born from her unwavering commitment to uncover the truth, protect her colleagues, and confront the entity that lurked in the shadows.

With each passing day, the weight of this responsibility grew, pressing upon her like a vice. Dr. Winters knew that she was their primary hope for understanding the entity's nature and, perhaps, finding a way to survive its malevolent influence. The narrative painted a vivid portrait of her internal struggles as she grappled with the immense task that lay before her. The fate of the team and the unknown horrors lurking within the facility rested squarely on her shoulders.

Chapter 7

Sinister Manifestations

Within the confines of the isolated research facility, the entity's sinister influence manifested in increasingly unsettling ways, as if the very walls of the cave itself bore witness to its ancient malevolence. Strange symbols etched themselves onto the walls, glowing with an eldritch light that seemed to seep from another dimension. These symbols danced with an eerie and unearthly grace, shifting and morphing as though they were alive. It was as though the very stone of the cave had been marked by an ancient and malevolent intelligence, leaving the team members in a state of unnerving fascination and dread.

Whispers filled the air, not mere sounds but incomprehensible mutterings that burrowed into the team's minds, leaving them on edge and sleepless. These whispers were a cacophony of voices, neither human nor animal, but something profoundly unsettling. They spoke in a language that transcended human understanding, conveying secrets and horrors that the team could not fathom. The voices seemed to come from all directions, creating a disorienting and nightmarish soundscape that grated on their sanity.

The manifestations were like a veil being slowly lifted, revealing the entity's dark nature, which defied human comprehension. Each discovery peeled away another layer of reality, revealing a darker and more nightmarish truth. The more they uncovered, the less they understood, and the more they feared the truth that lurked in the shadows.

The symbols, whispers, and eerie manifestations were puzzle pieces in a cosmic riddle that seemed designed to shatter their sanity.

The entity's attempts at communication grew more explicit, yet the messages it conveyed remained cryptic and ambiguous. It manifested in a myriad of ways, from eerie symbols and strange sounds to vivid, dream-like visions that danced at the edges of the team's consciousness. Each vision was a surreal nightmare, blurring the line between the waking world and the realm of the impossible. They saw glimpses of alien landscapes and monstrous, incomprehensible entities that haunted their dreams and waking hours. These visions were like windows into a dimension of cosmic horror, a place where the laws of reality no longer applied.

It sought to manipulate their perceptions, hinting at its ancient origins and cosmic significance. The team found themselves caught in a web of enigmatic riddles and unsettling, fragmented messages that felt like whispers from the abyss. The messages taunted them with the promise of forbidden knowledge and hinted at their insignificance in the face of the entity's cosmic power. The more they tried to decipher these messages, the more they felt like pawns in a game they could never hope to understand.

The realization that they were dealing with something far beyond their comprehension became increasingly evident. As they grappled with the entity's inscrutable intentions, their sense of unease and vulnerability deepened, intensifying the cosmic horror that had taken hold of their lives. The team had entered a realm where the laws of science and reason no longer applied, and they were at the mercy of an entity that existed beyond the boundaries of human understanding.

The team members, now fully aware of the entity's malevolent presence, found themselves caught in a web of escalating tensions and growing distrust. Every whispered word, every shadow cast by flickering lights, and every unexpected noise sent shivers down their spines. Trust was a rare commodity, and each team member began to question the others' motives. The mounting tensions within the group became a palpable force, as they struggled to comprehend the entity's power and the horrifying reality of their situation. The facility, once a bastion of scientific inquiry, had transformed into a battleground of fear and suspicion, and the entity's insidious influence continued to tighten its grip on their minds.

As the characters confronted the entity's insidious influence, they were forced to grapple with the profound limitations of their scientific knowledge. The very foundations of their understanding of the world had been shattered, and they found themselves in a realm where the rules of reality were no longer applicable.

The entity's cryptic messages, eerie manifestations, and disturbing visions had pushed them to the brink of sanity. They had delved into the heart of cosmic horror, where human comprehension faltered in the face of unimaginable forces. The entity, "The Whisperer in Ice," was an emissary of the Elder Gods, a cosmic entity of unfathomable power and significance. Their collective scientific expertise and intellect were dwarfed by the sheer magnitude of the unknown they now confronted.

A sense of existential dread pervaded their every moment. The boundaries of reality had blurred, and the characters were left with the horrifying realization that they were at the mercy of cosmic forces beyond their control. Their journey had taken them to a place where the universe itself seemed to conspire against their understanding. The concept of the unknowable loomed large in their minds, a daunting and relentless adversary.

In this chilling landscape, they found themselves caught between the relentless encroachment of the entity's influence and the limits of human perception. The once-sound pillars of science and reason had crumbled, leaving them adrift in a sea of cosmic uncertainty. Their battle for survival had entered a new phase, one where their greatest adversary was the very nature of the cosmos itself.

Chapter 8

Tensions Boil Over

The isolated research facility, once a place of scientific inquiry, had become a crucible of mounting fear and paranoia. The realization that they were confronting an incomprehensible entity, a cosmic force that defied all their knowledge, had pushed the team to their breaking point.

Tensions that had been smoldering beneath the surface now erupted like a volcano. The characters, who had once been colleagues, found themselves locked in a battle of wills, a desperate struggle for control and understanding.

As the realization of their dire predicament took hold, the atmosphere within the facility grew increasingly suffocating. The characters, each grappling with their own fears and insecurities, found it difficult to maintain the veneer of composure. The weight of their circumstances bore down upon them, and the strain was palpable.

The facility's confined spaces echoed with the rising conflicts, arguments, and emotional breakdowns among the team members. Friendships had shattered, trust had eroded, and each character faced the haunting question of who could be trusted in a world where cosmic horrors had become a chilling reality.

In this crucible of fear and uncertainty, they found themselves on the brink of madness, teetering on the edge of a precipice from which there might be no return. Their unity, once their greatest strength, had crumbled under the relentless pressure of the entity's malevolent influence.

The battle for survival had transformed into a battle against their own demons, a harrowing descent into the abyss of their own minds.

As tensions boiled over within the research facility, and the once-unified team descended into chaos, Dr. Evelyn Winters emerged as the unlikely beacon of hope. Despite the eroding trust and the cracks forming in their unity, she remained steadfast in her commitment to confront the entity that threatened to consume them all.

Dr. Winters, with her extensive background in Antarctic studies and her unyielding determination, took on the role of leader in this dire situation. Her colleagues, despite their doubts and fears, recognized that her expertise was their best chance at understanding and countering the entity's malevolence.

In the midst of the team's disintegration, Dr. Winters formulated a plan. Her strategy was grounded in science, but it also acknowledged the surreal and otherworldly nature of their adversary. She understood that to confront the entity, they would need to combine their scientific knowledge with an open-mindedness that defied the boundaries of reason.

While her team's cohesion faltered and trust remained a rare commodity, Dr. Winters' resilience shone through. She was determined to find a solution, to understand the entity's true nature, and to protect what remained of her team. It was a daunting task, but it was one she accepted with unwavering resolve, even as the world around them descended further into chaos and the malevolent entity continued to manipulate their every move.

As the team found themselves trapped within the confines of the isolated research facility, the erosion of trust among its members accelerated. The entity's relentless manipulations and their growing realization of its power were driving wedges between them, and the bonds that had once held them together were strained to the breaking point.

Suspicion and paranoia ran deep within the group as they grappled with the nightmarish idea that any one of them could be the entity's next unwitting host. The malevolent force lurking in their midst had shattered their sense of security, transforming the facility into a breeding ground for fear and mistrust.

Each team member's actions and words were scrutinized, every gesture and glance analyzed for signs of the entity's influence. The once-unified group had become a collection of isolated and desperate individuals, each struggling to distinguish friend from foe, as they faced a threat that transcended human understanding.

The entity's ability to exploit their deepest fears and vulnerabilities had turned their isolation into a crucible of paranoia. It was a psychological battle as much as a physical one, and the team members were beginning to understand that their survival depended not only on the entity's defeat but also on their ability to rekindle the trust they had lost. The path ahead remained treacherous, and the true nature of their adversary continued to elude them.

Chapter 9

The Unraveling Group

The group, which had once been tightly bound by a common goal and unwavering camaraderie, now stood on the precipice of disintegration. Their trust in one another had eroded, replaced by a growing sense of suspicion and unease. The entity's malevolent presence had sown the seeds of doubt within their minds, leaving them with a sense of isolation and hopelessness as they confronted the unknown horror lurking within the facility.

Each member of the team felt the weight of their fractured bonds, and the sense of unity that had once defined their purpose now seemed like a distant memory. The mounting conflicts, arguments, and emotional breakdowns among the group members reflected the profound strain on their relationships.

As their unity continued to fracture, the team was left with a grim understanding that their survival in the face of the entity's insidious influence might depend not only on their ability to confront this cosmic horror but also on their capacity to reconcile with each other. The path ahead remained treacherous and fraught with uncertainties, as they grappled with the entity's relentless manipulation and their own internal conflicts. It was a battle on multiple fronts, and the stakes could not have been higher.

Chapter 10

The Entity's Isolation

The entity's retreat into the shadows marked a turning point in the story. As it slithered away from the dying shell it had once inhabited, it left behind a gruesome reminder of the horrors that had unfolded within the research facility. The abandoned body, once a respected scientist, now lay contorted and lifeless, a grim testament to the entity's malevolent influence.

The team remained oblivious to the entity's cunning plan. They had witnessed the possessed scientist's decline, but they were unaware of the entity's escape. Their isolation within the research facility had heightened their paranoia, and their trust in one another had eroded to a fragile thread. The entity's decision to bide its time in the shadows only added to the atmosphere of dread that had enveloped the group.

The narrative now shifted its focus to the team's growing desperation. With the possessed scientist in a state of decay and the entity lurking in the shadows, the team faced a haunting realization. They were pawns in a cosmic game they couldn't comprehend, and their chances of survival were diminishing with each passing moment.

The entity's isolation within the facility marked the beginning of a new phase in the narrative, one that would bring the team face to face with their own vulnerabilities and the relentless malevolence of an entity that existed beyond the boundaries of human understanding. The story was hurtling toward a terrifying climax, where the entity's true nature would be unveiled, and the team's struggle for survival would reach its most harrowing point.

The team's growing awareness of the entity's nature had led to a crucial breakthrough. As they pieced together the unsettling puzzle of the entity's possession, they arrived at a chilling realization: the current host was none other than the possessed scientist, the one who had become a vessel for the entity's malevolence.

Their identification of the possessed scientist as the host was a turning point in their understanding of the entity's influence. It was a moment of clarity amidst the maddening chaos that had descended upon them. They had glimpsed the entity's method of survival – its ability to hop from one host to another when its current vessel had reached its limits.

Armed with this knowledge, the team felt a renewed sense of determination. They believed that by isolating the possessed scientist and ensuring their confinement, they could contain the entity's influence and potentially find a way to confront it. However, their unity was fragile, and the tension that had gripped them since the entity's awakening still lingered, threatening to tear them apart even as they faced this critical revelation. The team's next steps would be crucial, and their struggle to break free from the entity's insidious grasp was far from over.

The team's moment of relief quickly gave way to a horrifying realization. In a desperate attempt to convey the truth of their situation, the possessed scientist, in the throes of their deteriorating state, attempted to communicate with the team. Their words were a garbled mixture of cryptic messages and desperate pleas for understanding.

As the possessed scientist struggled to articulate their revelation, the team slowly pieced together the shocking truth: the entity had already moved on to a new host. The scientist was nothing more than a deteriorating vessel, a discarded shell that had served its purpose. The entity had cunningly abandoned the host, leaving behind a broken and hollow body.

The team, gripped by a paralyzing fear, had to confront the horrifying understanding that the entity was still among them. It had moved on, and they had no way of knowing who the new host might be. The entity was biding its time, lurking in the shadows, waiting for the opportune moment to strike once again.

The revelation sent shivers down their spines, as they realized that they were trapped in a nightmare where the line between reality and madness had become dangerously thin. The team's unity was now more crucial than ever, as they faced an entity that seemed one step ahead of their every move, a cosmic horror that defied comprehension and continued to weave its insidious web of terror.

The team was left in a state of desperation and dread, their unity shattered by the horrifying truth. Fully aware of the entity's insidious cycle, they faced the daunting task of confronting an enemy that could seamlessly transfer from host to host, leaving them in a state of perpetual vulnerability.

Desperation gnawed at their hearts as they grappled with the entity's cunning. It was a malevolent force that lurked among them, unseen and unpredictable. The fear that any one of them could become the entity's next host hung over their heads like a dark cloud.

Dread settled in their hearts as they realized that their situation had become increasingly dire. The entity's cycle of possession had placed them in a never-ending nightmare, where they were forever on the edge of a precipice, waiting for the entity to strike again. Their trust in each other had eroded, and they were left with a profound sense of vulnerability and isolation.

In the face of such overwhelming odds, the team had to muster every ounce of their courage and determination to confront an enemy that defied reason and science. The entity's insidious presence had plunged them into a cosmic horror beyond their wildest nightmares, and their fight for survival had become a battle against an adversary that seemed all but invincible.

Chapter 11

Dr. Winters' Discoveries

Dr. Evelyn Winters, in her relentless pursuit of understanding the entity, became the torchbearer of knowledge within the research facility. She delved deep into the forgotten annals of history, unearthing records of the ancient civilization that had once thrived beneath the Antarctic ice.

The texts she encountered were filled with cryptic symbols, the remnants of a culture that had sought communion with an outer god. Dr. Winters meticulously deciphered these symbols, slowly reconstructing the story of a civilization that had dared to make unholy pacts with cosmic entities.

As she pieced together the puzzle, she unveiled the entity's role as an emissary of the Elder Gods, a being of unimaginable power and cosmic significance. This revelation shook the very foundations of her scientific beliefs. She was no longer dealing with a mere scientific anomaly; she was confronting a force that existed beyond the comprehension of humanity.

The entity's connection to the outer god was a revelation that left Dr. Winters in a state of both awe and terror. It was as if she had opened a door to a dimension where reality itself was a malleable concept, and the laws of physics were but feeble guidelines. The understanding of their place in the universe crumbled before her, and the characters found themselves teetering on the precipice of existential horror.

As Dr. Winters continued her tireless research, the cosmic horror elements of the narrative deepened, and the characters grappled with the horrifying realization that they were pawns in a cosmic game far larger and more malevolent than they could have ever imagined. The boundaries of science and reason were shattered, leaving them in a reality where the unknown was vast, unfathomable, and deeply unsettling.

The realization of the entity's connection to the outer god sent shockwaves through the team. Dr. Evelyn Winters, in her tireless pursuit of knowledge, had unraveled a truth that transcended the boundaries of human understanding. The outer god, a deity of cosmic significance, was a being so vast and incomprehensible that it defied all conventional notions of divinity.

As Dr. Winters pieced together the puzzle, the team couldn't escape the overwhelming dread that permeated the research facility. The entity, once perceived as a sinister anomaly, now took on a far more ominous role as an emissary of this unfathomable cosmic entity. Their perception of reality began to fracture as they grappled with the implications of their situation.

The cosmic horror that had been a growing undercurrent in their lives now swelled to the forefront. The team was no longer battling a mere malevolent force; they were caught in a larger, cosmic struggle that stretched beyond the limits of human comprehension. Their knowledge, expertise, and scientific reasoning were rendered obsolete in the face of these cosmic forces.

The weight of their insignificance bore down upon them, and they questioned the very nature of their existence. Were they nothing more than unwitting pawns in a cosmic game, where humanity was an afterthought? The existential crisis that washed over them added another layer of horror to their already terrifying ordeal.

In this atmosphere of dread, they had to confront not only the entity but also their own vulnerability in the face of these colossal cosmic forces. Their struggle took on a new dimension, one that extended beyond the physical and into the metaphysical, where the very fabric of their reality was torn asunder, leaving them to grapple with the ultimate questions of existence in the face of insurmountable cosmic power.

Dr. Evelyn Winters' discoveries had shattered the illusion of humanity's dominance over the world and the universe. The entity's aspirations were nothing short of a cosmic cataclysm, a revelation that left the team grappling with profound existential dread.

As they delved deeper into the entity's cosmic ambitions, it became clear that the entity was not merely a malevolent force seeking to torment them. It was a harbinger of cosmic forces beyond human comprehension, a herald of the outer god's presence. The entity's role as an emissary of this unimaginably powerful deity struck terror into their hearts.

The team had unwittingly stepped into the crosshairs of a cosmic struggle, caught in a battle between an entity that sought to transcend its earthly limitations and an outer god whose existence defied the very laws of reality. The insignificance of humanity in the face of these cosmic forces was a bitter pill to swallow. They were but ants in the shadow of giants, their lives and struggles inconsequential on the grand stage of the cosmos.

The weight of their predicament was crushing, and they found themselves in a race against time and fate. The entity's megalomaniacal desires had set in motion a series of events that could lead to humanity's undoing. The team's understanding of their own vulnerability grew more profound, and they were forced to confront the stark reality that their very existence hung by a thread.

Dr. Winters' pursuit of knowledge had led them to the heart of a cosmic horror that defied reason, and as they grappled with the entity's aspirations, they found themselves teetering on the precipice of madness. The narrative embraced themes of existential dread, emphasizing the team's futile struggle against an unfathomable adversary, and the chilling revelation of their own insignificance in the face of cosmic forces beyond their control.

The team's understanding of the entity's cosmic origins and mega-lomaniacal aspirations plunged them into a bottomless abyss of cosmic horror. As the narrative unfolded, the sense of dread deepened, and they found themselves ensnared in a web of malevolence that transcended human understanding.

The implications of their situation were dire, a reality that now fully weighed upon them. They were no longer grappling with a mere horror confined to the icy depths of Antarctica. Instead, they had stumbled into the crossroads of cosmic forces that could reshape the very fabric of existence. The entity's aspirations to attain god-like status, with humanity as its unwitting stepping stone, cast a long, chilling shadow over their every thought and action.

With each revelation, their sense of impending doom grew more pronounced. The narrative painted a bleak picture of their future, one where they were trapped in a cosmic nightmare, aware of the entity's evolution and the horrors it would unleash upon the world. Their understanding of the entity's insidious cycle and cosmic significance intensified the overarching sense of cosmic horror that had consumed their lives.

They were no longer battling a tangible, comprehensible adversary. Instead, they found themselves on the front lines of a cosmic war, their meager existence inconsequential in the grand scheme of the universe. The narrative embraced the very essence of Lovecraftian Cosmic Horror, where the greatest terror lay in the unfathomable nature of the cosmic forces they had unwittingly awakened.

Chapter 12

The Entity's Internal Struggles

The entity's internal conflict grew more complex as it continued to transfer from host to host, each new experience bringing with it fragments of their humanity. Within the entity's malevolent consciousness, there were moments of regained humanity, brief and flickering like distant stars in the night sky.

During these fleeting moments, the entity would experience empathy, and a glimmer of understanding for the human condition would pierce through the dark shroud of its cosmic malevolence. It would witness the inner struggles, dreams, and fears of the host, gaining glimpses into their past and the lives they had led before becoming vessels for the entity's will.

These moments of regained humanity served to accentuate the entity's internal conflict. It was a being of both unfathomable cosmic power and the remnants of countless human souls. The duality within its consciousness, the struggle between the malevolent force and the fragments of humanity, added an additional layer of complexity to the narrative, deepening the sense of cosmic horror that pervaded the story.

The entity's internal turmoil, its occasional glimpses of humanity, and its ceaseless quest for god-like transcendence created a rich and multifaceted portrayal of an entity that was far more than a mere antagonist. It was a character in its own right, with its own internal conflicts and motivations, making it a central figure in the unfolding narrative.

As the entity continued to inhabit new hosts, its growing desire to survive became a central aspect of its character. It understood that the clock was ticking on each host's viability, and this realization intensified its determination to prolong its existence.

Within its cosmic consciousness, the entity developed a potent survival instinct, a primal urge to persist and transcend. It saw each new host as a lifeline, a vessel to carry it through the eons. The entity's will to survive was as powerful as its cosmic aspirations, and it would stop at nothing to ensure its continued existence.

This internal conflict, the struggle between its aspirations for godlike status and its primal need to survive, added a layer of complexity to the entity's character. It became a character defined by its relentless pursuit of both cosmic power and self-preservation, making it a formidable and multifaceted adversary for the team.

The entity's internal struggles and its unwavering will to survive became driving forces in the story, propelling the characters into a high-stakes battle against an entity that was as desperate as it was malevolent. This added depth to the cosmic horror that permeated the narrative, leaving the characters and readers alike with a chilling sense of dread and uncertainty.

As the entity continued to grapple with its internal conflict, its descent into madness became an increasingly prominent aspect of its existence. The dichotomy between its malevolent cosmic nature and the fragments of humanity it absorbed from its hosts created a tumultuous internal struggle, pushing the entity further down the abyss of insanity.

In moments of regained humanity, the entity experienced a fleeting empathy, an understanding of the human emotions and experiences it had absorbed. These brief respites from its malevolence served as haunting reminders of what it had once been, a cosmic entity corrupted by its insatiable thirst for power and cosmic significance.

The entity's growing madness manifested in erratic behavior and erratic decision-making. It would oscillate between moments of clarity, during which it recognized the consequences of its actions, and episodes of profound malevolence, where it pursued its cosmic aspirations at any cost. This internal struggle within the entity's psyche painted a picture of an entity torn between its cosmic ambitions and the remnants of its humanity.

The descent into madness was portrayed as a harrowing journey, as the entity's internal conflict intensified. The moments of empathy and understanding served as poignant glimpses into the cosmic entity's tragic existence, as it grappled with its own duality and the inevitable destination of its madness.

The entity's internal conflict was a tumultuous maelstrom of opposing forces, with its god-like aspirations pulling it in one direction and the remnants of its humanity tugging it in another. In the quiet recesses of its mind, the entity experienced moments of regained humanity that were marked by fleeting empathy and understanding. During these brief interludes, it could almost sympathize with the plight of the humans it had ensnared in its web of cosmic horror.

However, these moments of clarity were always fleeting, like candles flickering in the darkness of its malevolent soul. The entity's unquenchable desire to survive and achieve god-like status remained at the forefront of its consciousness. It recognized that the clock was ticking on each host's viability, and this awareness only intensified its determination to prolong its existence.

With every new host it inhabited, the entity absorbed more fragments of humanity, deepening the complexity of its internal struggles. The internal conflict became an integral part of its character, and readers could perceive the entity's fractured existence, teetering on the edge of sanity.

As the entity's descent into madness became more pronounced, it presented itself as an entity at war with itself. The narrative depicted its internal turmoil vividly, portraying it as a creature struggling to reconcile its malevolent nature with these fleeting glimpses of empathy. Its internal chaos was a driving force behind the narrative, creating an atmosphere of dread and uncertainty as the entity hurtled toward its inevitable evolution.

Chapter 13

A god like entity

The entity's transformation into a god-like being was a terrifying process, characterized by a profound change in its essence. It discarded the remnants of its human hosts, abandoning empathy and morality in favor of cosmic malevolence. Emerging from this metamorphosis, it became an entity that transcended human comprehension, a force with the ability to manipulate the very fabric of reality.

With its newfound power, the entity could warp time and space, harnessing cosmic forces that defied natural laws. Its presence alone distorted perception, leaving those who encountered it in a state of deep existential dread.

The entity's ambitions were equally horrifying. It aspired to destroy humanity and subjugate all existence to its will, viewing itself as the agent of cosmic chaos, a malevolent deity capable of reshaping the universe itself. Its goals were delusional, its desires insatiable, and its power unrivaled.

As the entity's transformation reached its zenith, the story entered a realm of cosmic horror that defied all understanding, where the characters and readers alike were confronted with a terror beyond imagination. The narrative now unfolded in a world where the struggle for survival and comprehension faced an even more urgent and dire threat, as the unleashed cosmic horrors challenged the very foundations of reality.

The frozen abyss of the subterranean cave echoed with the cosmic struggle, as Dr. Evelyn Winters and the survivors of the expedition confronted the entity, now transformed into a god-like, malevolent force. The air itself seemed to tremble with the weight of their impending clash.

The battle that ensued was a maelstrom of chaos, where the boundaries between reality and nightmare blurred. The very walls of the cave quivered as the entity unleashed its god-like power. Dr. Winters, armed with her knowledge and determination, stood as the last bastion of humanity's hope in this cosmic confrontation.

The very fabric of the universe strained under the entity's relentless assault. The survivors, battered and broken, refused to yield to the god-like being. Their every action was a testament to the indomitable spirit of humanity, as they struggled to defy the entity's apocalyptic aspirations.

It was a cataclysm of cosmic forces, a battle of wills that transcended the limits of human comprehension. The fate of not just the survivors but all of humanity hung in the balance, as they faced the ultimate test of their resilience and determination in the face of a god-like adversary.

The unleashed power of the entity shattered the fragile reality of the subterranean cave, plunging the research facility into a cataclysmic event of cosmic proportions. In that desperate hour, the characters found themselves pushed to the brink, their very existence hanging in the balance.

The facility's walls trembled and crumbled under the weight of the entity's god-like wrath. The air itself crackled with eldritch energy, and the survivors were engulfed in a tempest of chaos. Dr. Evelyn Winters, standing resolute, was a beacon of determination in the face of an apocalyptic tempest.

Amidst the chaos and devastation, the characters fought for their lives and, more significantly, for the fate of humanity itself. It was a battle that defied all reason, as they struggled against a god-like entity driven by delusional desires.

The unfolding cataclysm was a testament to the profound horror of facing a cosmic entity, and the apocalyptic consequences of its insatiable aspirations. In that dire moment, the characters were forced to confront the limits of their humanity, their willpower, and the grim reality that not all may emerge from this cosmic showdown unscathed.

As the cataclysmic showdown reached its climax, it left an indelible mark on the characters and the very essence of the story's cosmic horror themes. The research facility lay in ruins, a grim reflection of the havoc that had unfolded.

In the aftermath, the survivors found themselves forever changed, their minds scarred by the unfathomable horrors they had witnessed. Dr. Evelyn Winters, once a relentless seeker of knowledge, had glimpsed the abyss of cosmic forces beyond human understanding, leaving her haunted by the abyssal truths.

Yet, the entity's ultimate fate remained shrouded in enigma. It was as if the god-like being had slipped through the cracks of existence, leaving its destiny open to interpretation. The characters were left with a chilling sense of uncertainty, a lingering dread that the cosmic malevolence they had confronted may one day return, and the nightmare of the Arctic's ancient horrors may never truly end.

Chapter 14

Unresolved Mysteries

Amidst the smoldering remnants of the research facility, numerous mysteries and questions lingered like haunting specters in the minds of the survivors. The true extent of the entity's power, its cosmic ambitions, and the ultimate fate of such a god-like being remained shrouded in the deepest realms of uncertainty.

Dr. Evelyn Winters, burdened by the knowledge of the cosmic horrors she had confronted, found herself tormented by the enigmatic forces she had encountered. Her pursuit of understanding had led her to the precipice of madness, and now, even in the aftermath, she grappled with the eldritch truths that defied human comprehension.

The survivors huddled in the dim, flickering light of the facility's emergency lamps, their faces etched with both relief and the weight of the unknown. In whispered conversations that echoed with the lingering terror of their recent battle, they debated the entity's ultimate fate. Was it vanquished, or had it merely slinked back into the cosmic abyss, biding its time for a resurgence of unspeakable malevolence?

As the days turned to weeks and the survivors attempted to piece their lives back together, they couldn't escape the unsettling notion that the entity's malevolence may persist in the cosmic shadows, waiting for its moment to return and unleash horrors beyond imagination. The unresolved elements of their tale cast a pall of lingering intrigue and cosmic dread, reminding them that in the vast, unfathomable cosmos, some nightmares never truly end.

Dr. Winters, her mind forever scarred by the revelations of the entity's cosmic origins, found herself plagued by relentless visions of otherworldly landscapes and eerie, half-whispered secrets. She felt the weight of the unknown pressing down on her, driving her to the edge of sanity. Despite her determination to bring the entity's enigmatic aspirations to light, the eldritch truth remained just beyond her grasp.

The survivors too were haunted by the entity's legacy. Their nights were filled with unsettling dreams that blurred the line between reality and nightmare, and their waking hours were marked by a perpetual sense of unease. They knew that the entity's power was not something they could easily forget or dismiss. It had touched their lives in ways that defied explanation, leaving an indelible mark on their souls.

In the silence of their new reality, they couldn't help but wonder if the entity, with its god-like aspirations, had merely retreated temporarily, allowing them a brief respite before returning with even greater cosmic force. The survivors had peered into the abyss, and the abyss had peered back, leaving them forever changed by the experience, haunted by the cosmic mysteries that would forever remain unresolved.

As they contemplated the ambiguous conclusion of their harrowing ordeal, they were left with a profound sense of their own insignificance in the face of cosmic forces beyond human understanding. The entity's actions had revealed a malevolent intelligence that transcended mortal comprehension, and its ambitions had shaken the very foundations of their reality.

With the unresolved mysteries of their encounter lingering in the air like an unshakable shadow, the survivors knew that they could never return to their previous lives. They had crossed a threshold into a realm of cosmic horror, and the boundary between the known and the unknowable had been forever blurred. Whether the entity's influence would resurface or recede into the cosmic void remained uncertain, but one thing was clear: they were forever marked by the indescribable terrors they had faced, and their journey into the heart of a nightmare was far from over.

The survivors of the cataclysmic showdown found themselves united in the face of an uncertainty that clung to their every thought and action. The entity's god-like power and its delusional ambitions had left an indelible mark on their psyches, casting doubt upon their understanding of reality itself.

In the dimly lit remnants of the research facility, huddled together for both solace and safety, they exchanged hushed conversations that echoed with the haunting memories of their encounter with the cosmic horror. Dr. Evelyn Winters, once a beacon of knowledge and determination, now stared into the abyss of uncertainty with the rest of them. The cosmic mysteries that had been unearthed left her grappling with existential questions that had no clear answers.

As they gazed at the charred ruins of their once-scientific haven, a collective sense of vulnerability pervaded their thoughts. The entity's power had been unimaginable, its aspirations unfathomable. The survivors couldn't help but feel as though they had been granted a glimpse into the abyss of cosmic forces, and it had left them forever changed.

The conclusion of their harrowing ordeal remained shrouded in ambiguity. They debated whether the entity had been vanquished or had merely retreated, waiting in the cosmic shadows for an opportune moment to return. The survivors' lives had been irrevocably altered, and they had become witnesses to the enigmatic nature of the universe.

In the uncertainty of the aftermath, they pondered the far-reaching implications of the entity's existence and its cosmic significance. What did it mean for humanity to be so inconsequential in the face of such cosmic malevolence? The survivors were forced to confront the fragility of their existence and the limitations of human understanding.

As the survivors looked to the future, they couldn't escape the feeling that their encounter with the entity was but a glimpse into a universe teeming with cosmic horrors that defied explanation. The lingering uncertainty of their conclusion served as a haunting reminder that the boundary between reality and nightmare had been forever blurred. Their journey into the heart of a nightmare had left them with more questions than answers, inviting readers to contemplate the unfathomable depths of the cosmos and the lingering dread that comes with the unknown.

The survivors' journey into the heart of cosmic horror had left an indelible mark on their souls. As they stared into the abyss of the unknown, they couldn't help but reflect on the enduring legacy of the horrors they had witnessed. The cosmic forces that had once seemed distant and unimaginable had become an inextricable part of their lives.

The events at the research facility were seared into their memories, haunting their every thought and action. They had glimpsed the unfathomable depths of the cosmos, and it had left them forever changed. The knowledge that they were but insignificant beings in the face of such malevolent forces weighed heavily on their minds.

Even as they attempted to move forward with their lives, the survivors knew that the legacy of cosmic horror would forever be a part of them. The boundary between reality and nightmare had been forever blurred, and the unknown had become an ever-present specter, lurking in the corners of their consciousness.

The conclusion of their harrowing ordeal served as a stark reminder that the cosmic horrors they had encountered were not confined to the pages of a book. They were a part of the fabric of the universe, and their legacy would continue to cast a shadow over the survivors.

The enduring legacy of cosmic horror left room for interpretation and contemplation. The survivors couldn't escape the feeling that they were but witnesses to a vast and uncaring cosmos, where the line between reality and nightmare was a thin and fragile veil. The events they had experienced were a chilling reminder that the unknown would always be a part of their lives, waiting in the cosmic shadows to reveal its horrifying truths.

Chapter 15

Whispers in the Dark

The entity, a malevolent force that had laid dormant for eons, had found a vessel in the form of the possessed scientist. With each passing moment, its insidious influence over the scientist grew, like a creeping shadow that devoured the light.

The entity whispered nightmarish visions into the scientist's mind, weaving a tapestry of horrors that only they could see. It urged them to carry out its malevolent objectives, each directive more heinous than the last. The scientist, once a rational and brilliant mind, had become a pawn in the entity's sinister game.

The torment inflicted by the entity was psychological in nature, a slow and methodical degradation of the scientist's sanity. It was as if the entity reveled in the psychological anguish it could cause, savoring the descent into madness it had orchestrated.

The possessed scientist, haunted by the nightmarish whispers and driven by the entity's commands, became a living embodiment of horror. Their eyes held a vacant, distant gaze, and their actions were increasingly erratic and unhinged. The entity's influence had turned them into a marionette, dancing to the malevolent tune of an otherworldly puppeteer.

As the entity's torment deepened, it painted a chilling portrait of a once-brilliant mind succumbing to the darkness. The scientist's struggle was a harrowing one, as they battled the relentless onslaught of the entity's whispers in the dark, all while the rest of the team watched in helpless horror.

The entity's insidious presence had sewn the seeds of discord among the team members. They were no longer the unified group that had embarked on this expedition. Suspicion and paranoia had taken root, and each member found themselves grappling with their own internal conflicts.

Dr. Evelyn Winters, their once unwavering leader, was burdened by the weight of responsibility. She questioned her own judgment, constantly doubting whether her decisions were influenced by the entity's whispers. The internal conflict within her was a battle between her determination to protect her team and the fear that she might unknowingly be serving the entity's dark will.

Dr. Winters' second-in-command, Dr. Samuel Carter, found himself torn between loyalty and doubt. He had always trusted his colleagues implicitly, but now he couldn't help but wonder if one of them had already fallen under the entity's sway. His internal struggle was a relentless war between the desire to trust and the growing certainty that betrayal lurked within their midst.

Dr. Emily Hayes, an expert in ancient civilizations, grappled with her own inner demons. Her knowledge had led to the discovery of the entity's origins, and the weight of that knowledge weighed heavily on her conscience. She questioned her own role in awakening this cosmic horror, and her internal conflict revolved around the guilt and responsibility she felt for the team's plight.

The other team members, too, faced their own internal battles. Paranoia had seeped into every corner of their minds, and they struggled to distinguish between the entity's whispers and their own thoughts. Their individual conflicts were a reflection of the collective paranoia that had gripped the group, creating a web of uncertainty that threatened to tear them apart.

The entity's manipulation had not only unleashed horrors from the depths of Antarctica but had also torn at the fabric of trust that had once bound the team. As they grappled with their internal conflicts, the entity's presence loomed ever larger, a malevolent force that reveled in sowing discord and exploiting their growing sense of helplessness.

The once-cohesive group had now become a fragmented collection of individuals, their bonds strained to the breaking point by the entity's relentless psychological warfare. Trust, once the bedrock of their teamwork, had eroded, leaving in its wake a tense and suspicious atmosphere.

Dr. Evelyn Winters, who had once been the beacon of leadership and trust, now found her decisions met with skeptical glances and hushed murmurs. Her every action was scrutinized for signs of influence from the entity, and her once loyal team members questioned her motivations.

Dr. Samuel Carter, second-in-command and a close ally of Dr. Winters, became the subject of doubt as well. His past unwavering support for the team's leader was now viewed with suspicion. The group wondered if he, too, might be under the entity's sway, secretly working against their interests.

Dr. Emily Hayes, the expert in ancient civilizations who had unearthed the entity's origins, found herself the center of attention. Her knowledge had led them into this nightmare, and her colleagues couldn't help but wonder if she had withheld information or if her actions were guided by a hidden agenda.

The other team members were not exempt from the growing mistrust. Whispers and sidelong glances had become their new currency. Every member's actions were scrutinized, and every word analyzed for hidden meanings.

As the bonds that had once united them frayed further, a sense of isolation and unease settled over the group. The entity reveled in their disintegration, using their internal conflicts and distrust to its advantage. The once-strong team had become a collection of individuals, each questioning the loyalty and motivations of their colleagues. The fragile bonds that held them together were now perilously close to breaking, leaving them vulnerable to the entity's sinister influence.

The possessed scientist, once a respected member of the team, had become a shell of their former self under the relentless influence of the entity. Their descent into madness was unmistakable, and it sent ripples of fear and unease through the group.

As the days wore on, the scientist's actions grew increasingly erratic. They would mutter to themselves, their words a nonsensical jumble that sent shivers down the spines of those who overheard. In the dark corners of their room, they etched strange symbols onto the walls, symbols that seemed to pulse with an otherworldly glow, as if they were gateways to some unfathomable dimension.

The possessed scientist's eyes, once filled with intellect and reason, now held a manic gleam. They would frequently engage in bizarre rituals, lighting candles and chanting in languages no one could understand. Their behavior was so far removed from their former self that it was difficult to reconcile the two.

The other team members, watching the scientist's descent into madness, could not help but question their own sanity. Doubt gnawed at the edges of their minds. Was this madness contagious, or was it a result of the entity's malevolent influence?

As the internal struggles within the group intensified, the entity's hold on them tightened like a vice. The line between reality and delusion grew ever thinner, and they found themselves teetering on the precipice of madness. The once-rational scientists were now faced with the harrowing realization that they were sliding into a nightmarish abyss, their sanity slipping through their fingers like grains of sand.

Chapter 16

The Ties that Bind

The entity's manipulation ran deep, like insidious roots burrowing into the minds of the expedition members. It seized every opportunity to exploit the group's already fractured trust, skillfully fanning the flames of discord. Whispered conversations in the dimly lit corridors became hushed accusations, and sidelong glances were exchanged with growing suspicion.

As the entity's influence intensified, the characters' internal conflicts became increasingly pronounced. Dr. Evelyn Winters, once the stalwart leader of the group, found herself plagued by self-doubt. The entity's whispers had convinced her that some among her team were secretly working against her, conspiring to undermine her authority and take control of the situation. She struggled with the weight of leadership, fearing that her decisions might lead the team to ruin.

James, the team's geologist, had always been the optimist, but now he wrestled with doubt. He couldn't shake the feeling that there was a traitor in their midst, someone with sinister intentions. He constantly questioned his own judgment, wondering if he had been too quick to trust certain members of the team.

Sarah, the team's biologist, had grown increasingly paranoid. She watched her colleagues with a wary eye, wondering if any of them were infected by the entity's influence. The once-strong bonds of friendship among the team members had eroded, leaving Sarah feeling isolated and alone.

The possessed scientist, despite being a victim of the entity's control, struggled with their own internal conflict. They were acutely aware of the malevolent actions they were compelled to carry out, yet they were powerless to resist the entity's will. Each day, they grappled with guilt and despair, feeling like a prisoner in their own body.

The entity reveled in this chaos, manipulating the group like marionettes on strings. It whispered dark secrets and half-truths, stoking the fires of paranoia until they burned uncontrollably. Team members started questioning not only the intentions of their colleagues but also their own sanity.

The facility, once a place of scientific inquiry and collaboration, had become a breeding ground for fear and mistrust. The entity's ability to exploit the fractured trust within the group was a testament to its cunning and malevolence, and it left the team members teetering on the precipice of self-destruction, with no clear way to escape the web of deceit and paranoia that had ensnared them. Their internal conflicts, exacerbated by the entity's relentless manipulation, threatened to tear the group apart from the inside, leaving them vulnerable to the entity's insidious influence and the impending horrors that awaited them.

As the entity's influence continued to tighten its grip on the team, a palpable sense of isolation settled over the research facility. The characters, who had once been united by a shared sense of purpose and camaraderie, now found themselves adrift in a sea of doubt and suspicion.

Dr. Evelyn Winters, the team's leader, felt the weight of this growing divide most acutely. She had always been the one to rally her colleagues, to inspire them with unwavering determination and hope. But now, her attempts to keep the team together were met with skepticism and resistance. The doubts that plagued her mind were mirrored in the eyes of her team, eroding the trust that had once bound them.

James, the geologist, struggled to make sense of the rifts that had emerged within the group. He had always been the optimist, the one who believed in the power of teamwork. Now, he watched as his colleagues turned away from one another, unable to bridge the chasms of suspicion that had formed.

Sarah, the biologist, had withdrawn into herself. She had once been the peacemaker, the one who mediated disputes and offered a listening ear. Now, she had become withdrawn, unable to trust her own judgment, let alone the intentions of her fellow team members. The bonds of friendship that had once been the bedrock of their group had frayed, leaving Sarah feeling isolated and helpless.

The possessed scientist, trapped in a body not entirely their own, felt the growing divide most keenly. They knew that their presence was the catalyst for the team's disintegration, and the guilt weighed heavily on their shoulders. Each action they were compelled to carry out under the entity's influence further alienated them from their colleagues.

The research facility, once a sanctuary of scientific collaboration, had become a battleground of suspicion and despair. The characters' emotional turmoil was palpable, a reflection of the growing divide that threatened to tear them apart from the inside. Their inability to trust one another, coupled with the entity's relentless manipulation, left them isolated and vulnerable to the horrors that awaited them. The bonds that had once held them together were unraveling, and the characters were left to grapple with the devastating realization that their unity was slipping through their fingers, leaving them at the mercy of the entity's insidious influence.

Suspicion and paranoia had become the prevailing emotions within the group, infecting their interactions and casting a pervasive shadow over the once-united team. Each character had become a potential threat in the eyes of the others, and the entity's insidious influence had successfully sown the seeds of mistrust.

Dr. Evelyn Winters, who had once been the cornerstone of the team's unity, now found herself constantly second-guessing her own decisions. The weight of responsibility bore down on her, and every choice she made was met with skeptical glances and whispered doubts. She could feel the eyes of her colleagues on her, questioning her every move.

James, the geologist, couldn't shake the feeling that his fellow team members were harboring secrets. What were they really thinking? What dark intentions might lurk behind their actions? The trust he had once placed in his companions had eroded, replaced by a gnawing unease that left him perpetually on edge.

Sarah, the biologist, had withdrawn even further into herself, cocooned in a shell of self-preservation. She couldn't bring herself to trust anyone, not even James, with whom she had once shared a deep bond of friendship. The constant whispers and shifting shadows had left her in a state of perpetual paranoia.

The possessed scientist, caught in the maelstrom of mistrust, felt the weight of their colleagues' suspicion like a physical presence. They were a pariah, a source of contamination in the eyes of the others. The entity's influence had turned them into a living embodiment of fear and distrust.

Within the research facility, a suffocating atmosphere of isolation and unease had taken hold. Every whispered word, every shadow cast by flickering lights, and every unexpected noise sent shivers down their spines. Trust was a rare commodity, and each team member began to question the others' motives. The mounting tensions within the group had become a palpable force, as they struggled to comprehend the entity's power and the horrifying reality of their situation. The entity's influence, both psychological and social, had torn apart the bonds that had once united them, leaving them in a state of perpetual suspicion and paranoia, unable to escape the entity's relentless manipulation.

The unity that had once bound the team together was unraveling at an alarming rate. The entity's relentless manipulation had sowed distrust and suspicion among the characters, creating fault lines that threatened to tear them apart.

Dr. Evelyn Winters, the team's leader, found herself in the unenviable position of trying to hold the group together. She was acutely aware of the disintegration of their unity and knew that, without it, they were all vulnerable to the entity's insidious influence. Her determination to confront the malevolent force within the facility was matched only by her desperation to rebuild the trust that had eroded among her colleagues.

James, the geologist, was torn between his loyalty to the team and the overwhelming doubt that had crept into his mind. He grappled with the internal conflict of wanting to believe in his fellow team members but being unable to ignore the nagging suspicion that any one of them could be a puppet of the entity.

Sarah, the biologist, had withdrawn into a cocoon of self-preservation, and her attempts to reach out to her colleagues were met with frosty receptions. The internal conflict between her fear of the entity's influence and her yearning for human connection left her in a state of emotional turmoil.

The possessed scientist, once a vital member of the team, was now a pariah, shunned by their colleagues. The internal conflict they experienced, torn between their own humanity and the entity's malevolence, was a constant torment. They longed to be free of the entity's influence but felt increasingly trapped by its insidious grasp.

The disintegration of their unity left the team in a state of vulnerability. The atmosphere within the research facility was fraught with tension and distrust, and the characters faced the daunting task of not only overcoming the entity's influence but also rebuilding the fractured relationships that had once bound them. The despair that had settled over them was a palpable force, adding to the overall atmosphere of tension and unease as they grappled with their internal conflicts and the malevolent presence in their midst.

Chapter 17

Fractured Realities

The entity's insidious influence had reached a terrifying apex. It now toyed with the characters' minds, warping their perceptions of reality in ways that defied logic and reason. The research facility became a nightmarish landscape where the line between illusion and truth blurred to the point of nonexistence.

Dr. Evelyn Winters, the team's leader, was no longer certain of what was real and what was a product of the entity's torment. She found herself navigating a disorienting world where walls seemed to shift, corridors extended infinitely, and shadows danced with malevolent intent. The once-familiar environment had become a labyrinth of uncertainty.

James, the geologist, questioned the very ground he walked on. His once keen sense of direction had become useless in this altered reality. He struggled to maintain a grasp on what was genuine and what was a figment of the entity's manipulation. Each step he took filled him with trepidation, not knowing if the ground would remain solid beneath him.

Sarah, the biologist, found herself surrounded by grotesque distortions of nature. The flora and fauna that had once been her comfort now took on grotesque forms. She battled the internal conflict of wanting to cling to her scientific understanding of the world while grappling with the unnerving reality the entity imposed upon her.

The possessed scientist, caught in a perpetual nightmare, had become a puppet of the entity's warped reality. Their internal conflict between their own humanity and the entity's malevolence was exacerbated by the disorienting environment. They desperately sought a way to break free from the entity's nightmarish illusions.

The facility itself had transformed into a surreal and unpredictable realm. Rooms shifted and rearranged, corridors stretched endlessly, and the characters' own senses became unreliable. The entity's power to manipulate reality had plunged them into a nightmarish world where nothing could be trusted, and the line between illusion and truth had all but vanished.

In this surreal nightmare, the characters found themselves caught in a perpetual struggle to navigate an ever-shifting and disorienting world. What they had once taken for granted as reality had become a fragile concept, constantly slipping through their fingers.

Dr. Evelyn Winters, the team's leader, felt her grasp on sanity slipping as she moved through the facility's constantly changing corridors. The familiar walls and doorways seemed to rearrange themselves at the entity's whim. Every step she took became a leap of faith, as the line between genuine experiences and nightmarish delusions blurred into obscurity. The psychological torment of not knowing what was real and what was an illusion weighed heavily on her.

James, the geologist, experienced a profound sense of disorientation as he attempted to navigate the ever-shifting landscape. His internal compass, once a reliable tool, had become utterly useless. He struggled to differentiate between the distortions of the entity's reality and the genuine world he had known. The torment of living in a constant state of doubt and mistrust gnawed at his psyche.

Sarah, the biologist, found herself confronting grotesque distortions of the natural world. Her scientific understanding clashed with the nightmarish versions of plants and animals that surrounded her. Her internal conflict deepened as she attempted to cling to her knowledge of the real world while grappling with the overwhelming uncertainty of this surreal landscape.

The possessed scientist, a mere pawn in the entity's cruel game, was trapped in a nightmarish existence. Their own internal conflict between their fading humanity and the malevolence of the entity was intensified by the distorted reality in which they were ensnared. Every step they took, every shadow they saw, was a source of torment as they desperately sought to distinguish between what was real and what was a creation of the entity's sadistic mind.

Their psychological torment was unrelenting as they grappled with the ever-changing, distorted world around them. Their sense of reality had become a fragile construct, and the line between genuine experiences and nightmarish delusions continued to blur, pushing them to the brink of madness.

As the entity continued to warp their reality, the characters felt their sanity slipping away with each new distortion. It was as though they were teetering on the precipice of madness, desperately trying to maintain a semblance of control over their unraveling minds.

Dr. Evelyn Winters, once a pillar of rationality and logic, now found herself questioning the very nature of reality. The constant distortions of the world around her eroded her confidence in her own perceptions. Every step she took, every object she touched, seemed to taunt her with its unreliability. Her desperate attempts to make sense of her surroundings were like grasping at smoke, and the relentless assault on her sanity left her feeling like a stranger in her own mind.

James, the geologist, grappled with a growing sense of disconnection from the world he had known. His understanding of the natural order was shattered as the entity's distortions played tricks on his senses. He could no longer trust the stability of the ground beneath his feet or the consistency of the walls around him. His grip on reality slipped further with each passing moment, and he felt as though he were losing his very sense of self.

Sarah, the biologist, struggled to reconcile her scientific knowledge with the grotesque distortions of the natural world that surrounded her. The entity's reality warp had turned her understanding of biology into a nightmarish puzzle with pieces that refused to fit together. Her attempts to maintain her sanity were a constant battle against the overwhelming uncertainty that pervaded her every thought.

The possessed scientist, a tragic figure in this cosmic horror, was trapped in a nightmarish existence where their fading humanity clashed with the malevolence of the entity. The constant shifting of reality only intensified their internal conflict, pushing them closer to the brink of madness. Every moment spent in the distorted world was a torment, and they struggled to retain a shred of their own identity.

Their deteriorating grip on sanity was palpable, and their desperate attempts to make sense of their surroundings and maintain their mental faculties added to the overarching sense of dread that permeated their nightmarish ordeal.

The world around them had become a shifting, surreal nightmare where nothing could be trusted. The entity's relentless manipulation of reality had created a disorienting and chaotic landscape, pushing them deeper into a realm of cosmic horror.

Every step they took, every door they opened, seemed to lead to a different, distorted version of their research facility. The walls pulsed and shifted, and the very ground beneath them seemed to writhe with an unnatural energy. Time itself appeared to lose meaning as the environment twisted and contorted before their eyes.

Their senses, once reliable instruments of perception, had become untrustworthy. The colors of the walls would shift, objects would morph into grotesque parodies of themselves, and the air was thick with an otherworldly resonance. The very concept of reality had fractured, leaving them in a perpetual state of uncertainty.

As the events unfolded, the characters grappled with an existential dread that gnawed at the core of their being. They questioned the nature of reality itself, unsure of what was real and what was a product of the entity's malevolence. The line between sanity and madness had blurred, and they were trapped in a nightmarish world where the boundaries of their own perception had dissolved.

The sense of existential dread grew with each passing moment, and they were left with a profound and horrifying realization. They had become pawns in a cosmic game, their very existence hanging by a thread in a world where the rules of reality had been rewritten by an entity of unfathomable power.

Chapter 18

A Descent into Madness

The entity's relentless torment knew no bounds. It was as though their minds had become a canvas for the entity's dark artistry, and every stroke of psychological manipulation pushed them closer to the brink of madness.

The torment was unrelenting, a ceaseless assault on their sanity. It whispered nightmarish visions into their minds, twisted their perceptions of reality, and played upon their deepest fears and insecurities. The entity reveled in their suffering, its sadistic delight driving them further into the abyss of insanity.

As the torment escalated, their descent into madness became more pronounced. They could no longer trust their own thoughts, their own senses. The world had become a nightmarish labyrinth of delusion, and they were trapped in its ever-shifting corridors.

They felt as though they were teetering on the edge of a precipice, their grasp on sanity slipping with each passing moment. The entity's psychological onslaught was an unrelenting force, an unending nightmare that threatened to consume them entirely. They were locked in a battle for their own minds, and the outcome was uncertain, as the entity's power to drive them to madness seemed boundless.

Their internal struggles mirrored the entity's descent into madness. It was as though they were locked in a nightmarish dance, a macabre waltz where the steps were dictated by the entity's insidious influence.

As they grappled with their own demons and the entity's unrelenting torment, they found themselves caught in a battle of wills that transcended the bounds of the physical world. It was a battle that raged within the recesses of their minds, a relentless struggle for control over their own sanity.

Their deteriorating mental states became increasingly apparent. The lines between reality and delusion blurred, and the boundaries of their own identities began to fray. They could no longer discern where their own thoughts ended and the entity's manipulations began.

The entity's influence had burrowed deep into their psyches, and the battle of wills played out on the stage of their consciousness. It was a battle that left them teetering on the precipice of madness, their minds a battleground where the entity's malevolent whispers and their own dwindling sanity clashed in a nightmarish crescendo.

They found themselves locked in a harrowing battle with their own fractured minds. Each one was forced to confront their deepest fears, anxieties, and traumas, all of which the entity wielded as weapons against them.

The entity's influence had a way of unearthing the darkest corners of their psyches, exposing long-buried wounds and insecurities. It was as if the malevolent force had access to a repository of their most intimate and tormenting experiences, and it used them to fuel the psychological warfare it waged.

As they grappled with the entity's relentless assault on their sanity, they were also compelled to face the darkness within themselves. The emotional turmoil was relentless, as they fought not only against the entity's manipulations but also against the demons that lurked in the recesses of their own minds.

Their personal demons, which had long been suppressed, rose to the surface. Memories of past traumas, insecurities, and regrets became vivid and haunting. They were forced to relive moments they had tried to forget, and the emotional pain was a torment all its own.

In the battle against the entity, they discovered that they were also battling the complex tapestry of their own psyches. It was a war on two fronts, one against an external malevolence and another against the inner demons that had long haunted them. The psychological toll was immeasurable, and the line between the real and the unreal continued to blur as they navigated the treacherous terrain of their fractured minds.

The relentless torment inflicted by the entity continued to push them to the limits of their psychological endurance. Each day brought new trials, new horrors, and new nightmares that tested the very fabric of their sanity.

They struggled desperately to maintain a grip on their mental faculties in the face of an adversary that seemed to revel in their suffering. The entity's malevolence knew no bounds, and it exploited every weakness, every fear, and every vulnerability they possessed.

As the events unfolded, the weight of their internal battles became as daunting as the external threat posed by the entity. They faced the harrowing reality that their own minds had become battlegrounds, and the line between their own thoughts and the entity's influence was increasingly blurred.

Despair hung heavy in the air, and their psychological endurance was stretched to its breaking point. The relentless torment was unyielding, and they grappled with the profound fear that their descent into madness was a fate they could not escape. The line between reality and delusion continued to fade, and the entity's power over their minds grew stronger with each passing moment.

Chapter 19

The Shadows Within

As the entity's influence continued to tighten its grip, they were forced to confront the darkest aspects of their own psyches. The malevolent entity's psychological manipulation skillfully exposed their innermost fears and insecurities, laying them bare for all to see.

Their fears varied, as did their sources. For one, it was a traumatic childhood experience that had long haunted their dreams. For another, it was the gnawing insecurity about their worth in the eyes of their colleagues. Yet another was tormented by the guilt of a past decision that had cost lives.

The entity was relentless in its torment, bringing these deeply buried fears to the forefront of their consciousness. It was as if the entity had the ability to reach into the deepest recesses of their minds and pluck out their most vulnerable and fragile moments, then dangle them before their eyes like a cruel puppeteer.

This unearthed vulnerability made them increasingly raw and exposed. The facade of composure they had maintained for so long crumbled, and they were left to grapple with their inner demons in the harsh light of day. They couldn't escape the relentless onslaught of their own vulnerabilities, and the boundaries between their thoughts and the entity's manipulations grew ever more porous.

Their internal struggles became as daunting as the external cosmic horror they faced. The line between their own fears and the horrors that resided within themselves blurred, leaving them in a perpetual state of inner turmoil. They not only had to confront the malevolent entity that lurked in the shadows but also reckon with the shadowy depths of their own psyches.

The entity's psychological assault knew no bounds. It was a relentless, remorseless adversary that exploited their vulnerabilities and weaknesses with chilling precision. It left them no refuge, no sanctuary from their own anxieties and traumas. Every waking moment was a battle, and the entity was a ruthless enemy that knew their innermost fears all too well.

Their vulnerabilities were many and varied, and the entity weaponized them with cruel efficiency. For one, it was a gnawing fear of abandonment, a deep-seated anxiety that they were destined to be alone. The entity magnified this fear, whispering in their ears that they were truly isolated in this hellish place, with no hope of rescue.

For another, it was an old trauma, an incident that had left them scarred and broken. The entity dragged them back to that nightmarish moment, replaying it in their mind like a never-ending horror film, each time with a more gruesome twist.

Their insecurities were also laid bare. The entity reveled in making them doubt their own worth, convincing them that they were unworthy of the respect and admiration of their colleagues. It taunted them with the idea that they were merely impostors, pretending to be something they were not.

This unrelenting torment intensified the atmosphere of dread and despair that hung over them like a shroud. They were trapped not only in a physical sense within the research facility but also in a psychological nightmare of their own making. The entity's psychological assault left them on the precipice of their own sanity, teetering on the edge as they grappled with their emotional turmoil.

The battle they faced was not just against a malevolent external force; it was a profound conflict within themselves. Their minds had become battlegrounds where their inner demons clashed with their resilience, a battleground where the entity's manipulations ran deep.

Each day was a struggle to retain their sanity and sense of self. The entity's relentless whispers and nightmarish visions had worn down their psychological defenses. They fought against the haunting memories that the entity dragged from the recesses of their minds, memories of past traumas and regrets. These inner demons clawed at the edges of their consciousness, threatening to overwhelm them.

Their sense of identity had been eroded by the entity's psychological assault. They questioned their own thoughts, wondering if the doubts and fears that plagued them were their own or the insidious whispers of the entity. It was a battle not only for their sanity but for the very essence of who they were.

Amid this internal conflict, they attempted to resist the entity's influence. They clung to shreds of their former selves, desperately trying to find a foothold in the chaos of their own minds. It was a battle they could not afford to lose, for if they succumbed to the entity's manipulations, there would be no coming back from the abyss of madness.

The internal struggle was as daunting as the external threat posed by the entity. It was a battle they fought in silence, a battle that raged within the depths of their psyches. The entity had become not just an external adversary but a sinister puppeteer, orchestrating a descent into madness that knew no bounds.

The darkness within them was like a yawning abyss, an uncharted realm of emotional vulnerabilities and psychological wounds. The entity's relentless influence had laid bare these inner demons, exposing them to a level of horror they had never before imagined.

In the depths of their souls, they confronted their own fears, insecurities, and past traumas. Memories long buried had resurfaced, vivid and tormenting. The entity's manipulation had a way of targeting their weakest points, exploiting their deepest anxieties, and tearing open old wounds. It was as if their own minds had become instruments of torment, playing a symphony of anguish that echoed through the very core of their being.

Each day, they found themselves grappling with these inner shadows, and the struggle had become as daunting as the external threat posed by the entity. They were trapped in a nightmarish dual battle, fighting not only to survive the entity's influence but also to retain their own sense of self.

Hopelessness settled like a heavy shroud over their hearts. They had come to terms with the fact that this battle was not only about confronting an external malevolent force; it was also a harrowing journey into the darkness that resided within them. The entity had succeeded in unearthing their deepest fears and insecurities, turning them into unwitting weapons against themselves.

In this profound darkness, they realized that they had to confront not only the external entity but also the demons that lurked within. The horror had reached a level where the line between their own psyche and the entity's influence had blurred, and they were left to navigate this treacherous terrain with a growing sense of despair. The battle was no longer just against an external foe; it had become a battle for their own souls.

Chapter 20
Lost in Time and Space
Reality itself had become a malleable, shifting entity under the influence of the malevolent force that had taken root within the research facility. The entity's power had reached such heights that it could now distort the very fabric of time and space, leaving them in a disorienting and surreal environment where the laws of reality no longer applied.

They moved through a world that defied comprehension, where cause and effect were no longer reliable guides. Time twisted upon itself, moments overlapping in chaotic disarray. Spaces folded in on each other, creating impossible geometries that defied the rational mind. The very ground beneath their feet seemed to ripple and churn, as if they walked on the surface of a living, breathing entity.

The entity's manipulation of time and space left them in a constant state of disorientation. What they once considered the laws of the universe were now mere suggestions, easily overwritten by the entity's unfathomable power. The concept of past, present, and future became blurred, and they found themselves in a perpetual state of uncertainty.

In this surreal landscape, they struggled to maintain a grip on their sanity. Every step they took, every decision they made, was a venture into the unknown. The entity's ability to warp reality added an additional layer of cosmic horror to their already dire circumstances, pushing them deeper into a world where the boundaries of existence had lost all meaning.

In this distorted realm where time and space were ever-shifting, they found themselves in a perpetual state of disarray. The passage of time became a fluid concept, as moments flowed into one another without warning. They might take a step forward and find themselves inexplicably transported to a place that seemed eons in the past or projected into a future they couldn't comprehend.

Spatial dimensions were equally capricious. Hallways stretched into infinity, folding in on themselves, and doors led to places that defied logical connection. The very architecture of the facility seemed to mock their attempts to navigate it, as if the building itself had become an extension of the entity's will.

Amidst this chaos, they struggled to maintain a sense of direction and purpose. What had once been familiar corridors and rooms were now alien landscapes, their understanding of the world fragmented. Each step they took was a gamble, as they had no way of predicting where it would lead them.

Their vulnerability to the entity's cosmic machinations was laid bare in this shifting reality. They could no longer rely on the laws of the physical world to guide them. The entity's manipulation of time and space left them in a constant state of uncertainty, and they grappled with the profound challenge of adapting to a world where the very foundations of reality had been upended.

In the distorted reality where time and space were mere playthings of the entity, the cosmic horror that had enveloped them reached new depths. The very foundations of their understanding of existence had crumbled, leaving them adrift in a sea of existential terror.

As they struggled to navigate this surreal and nightmarish landscape, they were confronted with the overwhelming insignificance of humanity in the face of cosmic forces that defied comprehension. The rules that had governed their lives, the constants that had given them a sense of security, were now shattered. They were but motes of dust in a universe that cared nothing for their existence.

The entity's manipulation of time and space served as a stark reminder of their vulnerability in the grand scheme of things. They grappled with the unsettling realization that they were at the mercy of powers far beyond their control, powers that regarded them with indifference at best and malevolence at worst.

Each moment in this disorienting reality deepened the cosmic dread that had taken hold of them. They were not merely battling a malevolent entity; they were battling the very fabric of the cosmos itself. The rules of their existence had been rewritten, and in this maddening new world, they could do nothing but confront the profound insignificance of their own existence.

In the ever-shifting and unpredictable reality created by the entity, they felt their grasp on logic and reason slipping away. It was as if the very fabric of the universe had unraveled, leaving them adrift in a maddening sea of cosmic absurdity. Their once-sturdy sense of self was fractured, and they struggled to maintain their sanity in a world where the laws of existence no longer applied.

As the entity's cosmic influence reached new heights, the atmosphere of existential horror became almost palpable. They were faced with the stark realization that they were powerless in the face of forces that transcended human understanding. The very notion of what was real and what was illusion had become a blurred, indistinct line, and they were left with a haunting sense of disorientation.

The events closed with a lingering dread that clung to them like a shroud. They were trapped in a reality that mocked their feeble attempts to comprehend it, a reality where the very concept of self and sanity seemed fragile and fleeting. In this world of endless uncertainty, they grappled with the unsettling notion that they were at the mercy of forces beyond human reckoning, and the existential horror that had plagued them throughout their ordeal had reached its zenith.

Chapter 21

Echoes of the Past

In the cryptic whispers of the entity, fragments of the ancient civilization's history began to unfold. They were granted glimpses into the advanced humanoid society that had once thrived in the frigid expanse of Antarctica. The entity served as a living repository of this civilization's collective memories, offering them tantalizing insights into the enigmatic culture that had once called this frozen wasteland home.

These revelations were like shards of a shattered mosaic, providing glimpses into the civilization's vast reservoir of knowledge and technology. They marveled at the sophistication of this ancient society, which had harnessed the harsh environment to create marvels that defied their understanding. The secrets of the past were gradually unveiled, allowing them to piece together the civilization's reverence for the outer god and the dire consequences that had befallen them as a result.

The entity's role as a bridge to this forgotten world added a layer of cosmic intrigue to their already harrowing journey, as they grappled with the weight of the ancient knowledge they were now privy to. The echoes of the past resonated with the present, intertwining their fates with those who had once walked this desolate landscape.

In the eerie whispers and visions revealed by the entity, the grim history of the ancient civilization unfurled before their eyes. They were forced to confront the unspeakable horrors and calamities that had led to the civilization's harrowing downfall. The chilling details of their demise painted a picture of cosmic dread and inescapable doom.

The tales they heard were ones of unspeakable atrocities and malevolent forces that had clawed at the civilization's very soul. It was a society plagued by madness, consumed by dark rites, and ultimately torn asunder by the influence of the outer god they had worshipped. The consequences of their hubris were catastrophic, and the civilization had paid a terrible price for seeking to harness the power of the cosmic entity.

As they delved deeper into this macabre history, the characters grappled with the overwhelming sense of cosmic dread that enveloped them. They couldn't help but draw unsettling parallels between the ancient civilization's fate and their own predicament, a stark reminder of the malevolent forces that lurked in the cosmic shadows. The horrors of the past echoed ominously in the present, intensifying the sense of inevitable doom that hung over them like a shroud.

As the entity unveiled the secrets of the ancient civilization, they found themselves wrestling with a multitude of questions and doubts. The newfound knowledge painted a complex and chilling portrait of the entity's motivations and its connection to the outer god worshipped by the long-lost society.

They couldn't help but wonder if the entity's actions were guided by a desire to follow in the footsteps of the outer god, seeking to attain god-like status at the expense of humanity. The implications of this revelation weighed heavily on their minds, and they were left to contemplate the entity's role in the civilization's catastrophic downfall.

The entity's insatiable thirst for power and its willingness to manipulate the ancient civilization for its own ends left them with a profound sense of dread. They had become unwitting pawns in a cosmic game, ensnared by forces beyond human comprehension. The lines between humanity and cosmic entities blurred, and they grappled with the horrifying understanding that they were mere playthings in a malevolent cosmic design.

As they delved deeper into the entity's motivations and cosmic significance, the story's themes of cosmic horror grew in depth and complexity. The characters found themselves on a treacherous path, navigating the thin line between knowledge and madness, as they sought to uncover the truth about the entity's intentions and their own place in the cosmic order.

With each revelation the entity unveiled, the narrative grew more intricate, weaving a complex tapestry of cosmic horror. The layers of complexity deepened as they grappled with the consequences of their newfound knowledge, standing on the precipice of a profound mystery that seemed to expand infinitely before them.

The entity's revelations had opened doors to a world of enigma and intrigue, leaving them with more questions than answers. They were caught in a web of uncertainty, unable to discern the entity's true motivations and the extent of their own involvement in the unfolding cosmic drama.

As the events of the narrative unfurled, the unease that had been present throughout reached its zenith. Their attempts to decipher the entity's intentions and their own place in the cosmic order only led to further ambiguity. The story's conclusion left them in a state of disquiet, with the understanding that they were entangled in a cosmic web of horror, their path fraught with uncertainty and their journey into the unknown far from over.

Chapter 22

The Breaking Point

With each passing moment, their grip on sanity grew increasingly tenuous. The unrelenting torment inflicted by the entity, its psychological manipulations, and the unyielding weight of cosmic horrors had pushed them to the very brink of their endurance.

Their minds, once resilient and rational, were now fragile and frayed. They teetered on the edge of a precipice, the chasm of madness beckoning with each nightmarish vision and each whisper from the entity. The breaking point had been reached, and the fragility of their sanity was laid bare for all to see.

As events unfold, it painted a harrowing picture of their internal turmoil, a tumultuous landscape where reason and madness warred for dominance. They were left to grapple with the torment that had brought them to this precipice, knowing that the abyss of insanity loomed just beyond their shattered resolve.

Their descent into madness was a gradual and agonizing process, marked by the unrelenting psychological torment inflicted by the entity. With each passing day, their mental states deteriorated, and the nightmarish quality of their experiences grew more pronounced.

The lines between reality and delusion blurred, and they found themselves trapped in a nightmarish labyrinth of the mind. Their thoughts, once rational and ordered, now spiraled into chaotic maelstroms of fear and paranoia. The world around them twisted and contorted, taking on grotesque and surreal forms that defied all logic.

Every waking moment was a battle to retain a semblance of sanity, a struggle against the malevolent influence that delighted in their suffering. They clung to their last shreds of reason, desperately trying to make sense of a world that had become a fractured and disorienting nightmare. But with each passing day, the abyss of madness yawned wider, threatening to swallow them whole.

The impending sense of doom intensified, casting a long and suffocating shadow over them. They were trapped in a nightmarish reality, a world where the boundaries of their own minds had become prisons, and there was no respite from the unrelenting influence of the entity.

Every day brought new terrors, new distortions of their perceptions, and new depths of psychological torment. The feeling of hopelessness loomed over them like a heavy, inescapable fog. They had come to terms with the fact that their mental states were fragile, teetering on the edge of the abyss, and there seemed to be no way to break free from the entity's malevolence.

The events closed with a chilling atmosphere of dread and despair. The world they once knew had crumbled into a nightmare, and the entity reveled in their suffering, driving them further into the depths of madness. The future looked bleak, and the darkness that surrounded them was unyielding, a relentless force that seemed impossible to overcome.

25

Chapter 23

The Abyss Gazes Back

As the weight of their existential crisis bore down upon them, the very foundations of their understanding crumbled. They found themselves adrift in a vast cosmic sea, where the familiar shores of reason and comprehension had been swallowed by an abyss of unknowable proportions.

The entity's god-like aspirations cast a long, dark shadow over their sense of self. It was as if they had been given a fleeting glimpse into the mind of a deity, one with ambitions that spanned across the fabric of existence. It was a revelation that left them feeling minuscule, their aspirations, struggles, and achievements reduced to mere whispers in the cosmic wind.

In the face of such overwhelming power and malevolence, they questioned the validity of their reality. The very concept of self, once a stable anchor in their lives, became a fragile construct. They grappled with the disconcerting notion that their thoughts, their actions, and their very existence were but grains of sand in the endless cosmic desert.

Their existential torment intensified as they tried to make sense of this newfound knowledge. The entity's revelations had torn away the comforting veil of ignorance that had shielded them from the horrors of the cosmos. They were left in a state of despair, as the once-solid ground of their understanding turned into a shifting, treacherous quicksand of uncertainty.

Events closed with a profound sense of cosmic horror, as they faced the chilling truth that the universe was an unfathomable and uncaring entity. Their lives, their existence, and their suffering were inconsequential in the grand tapestry of the cosmos, and they were left to grapple with the terrifying reality of their own cosmic insignificance.

The events exploration of cosmic horror themes reached its zenith as they delved deeper into the entity's nature and its connection to the outer god. They were faced with revelations that transcended human comprehension, and the realization that some truths were simply too terrible to bear.

The incomprehensible nature of the entity became an ever-present specter, a lurking dread that whispered in the darkest corners of their minds. Its cosmic significance was a weight that pressed upon their souls, a reminder of their own insignificance in the grand scheme of the universe.

As the events unfolded, the cosmic horror elements intensified, casting a long, dark shadow over their futile struggle. The story became a relentless descent into existential terror, where the boundaries of reality and sanity blurred into a nightmare landscape of unimaginable proportions.

The very core of their being trembled as they grappled with the enormity of the entity's power and its connection to the outer god. It was a revelation that shattered their understanding of the world, leaving them in a state of perpetual dread. The story emphasized that in the face of such cosmic malevolence, humanity was but a speck of dust in the vast, indifferent cosmos, and their struggle against the entity was a futile endeavor.

The cosmic dread that permeated the story left a lasting impression, underscoring the profound horror of facing an adversary beyond human understanding. It was a narrative that plunged them into the abyss of the unknown, where the most terrible truths lay hidden, and where the boundaries of reality and sanity dissolved into a maddening void.

Their struggle against the entity reached a point of futility that seemed insurmountable. Their efforts to resist its influence and decipher its cosmic significance were like trying to hold back the tide with bare hands. The more they fought, the more they realized the hopelessness of their endeavors.

With a heavy heart and a profound sense of resignation, they grappled with the notion that they were mere mortals, and the entity's power was as boundless as the cosmos itself. Their attempts to comprehend the entity's motives and thwart its malevolent plans were akin to shouting into the void, with no assurance that anyone or anything was listening.

As events unfolded, the story drove home the hopelessness of their situation, painting a picture of existential dread and despair. It was a narrative that forced them to confront the limits of their understanding and the harsh truth that they were powerless in the face of forces that defied human reason and control.

26

Chapter 24

The Final Revelation

The tension had been steadily building, and at last, events reached their climactic moment. The time for a final, desperate confrontation with the entity had come. With a deep understanding of the catastrophic threat the entity's evolution posed to humanity, they knew they had to act swiftly and decisively. The stakes were at their highest, and the outcome of this confrontation would determine the fate of not only their team but all of humanity.

As the climactic confrontation unfolded, a chilling revelation loomed on the horizon. The events that transpired left the ultimate fate of them and the entity shrouded in ambiguity. The conclusion was marked by a profound sense of uncertainty, casting a long shadow of cosmic horror over the narrative. They were left to grapple with the unsettling notion that the entity's malevolent influence might persist, lurking in the shadows, awaiting the opportune moment to strike again. The story concluded with an eerie sense that the cosmic horrors they had faced were far from over, and the true extent of the entity's power remained an enigma.

The culmination of their harrowing journey in the face of the entity's malevolence reinforced the story's overarching themes of cosmic horror. It underscored the notion that certain truths were too dreadful for the human mind to fully grasp, that some mysteries were best left unsolved. The revelation of the entity's cosmic significance and its connection to the outer god evoked an overwhelming sense of existential dread. They came to understand, with a shiver down their spines, that humanity was ultimately insignificant in the grand tapestry of the cosmos. Their struggles against the entity had been a futile endeavor, a mere flicker of resistance in the face of unfathomable forces that cared naught for the plight of mortals. The themes of cosmic horror resonated with a chilling resonance as they grappled with the profound insignificance of humanity in the cosmic scheme of things.

The story closed with an atmosphere of uncertainty and dread, a palpable sense of unease that lingered in the minds of its readers. It left them with haunting questions and a chilling awareness of the unknown. The horrifying possibilities that lay beyond the narrative's conclusion remained shrouded in cosmic mystery, leaving a lingering sense of cosmic horror that refused to dissipate. The chilling finale dared readers to contemplate the abyss, to peer into the void of the unknown, and to confront the harrowing truth that some horrors were best left untouched, their full extent forever hidden in the shadows of the unimaginable.

27

Epilogue

The Obsessed Hunter

I've spent my entire life in the Alaskan wilderness, honing my skills as a hunter and surviving the harshest of conditions. But that fateful journey into the heart of the wilderness changed everything. It began with a chilling whisper in the frigid wind, an otherworldly voice that seemed to call out to me from the depths of the forest. It was an eerie, inhuman presence that I couldn't ignore.

At first, I was unnerved, but I couldn't resist the allure of the mysterious entity that seemed to guide me. I became convinced that it held the key to unraveling the secrets of the cosmos. Day by day, my obsession with this entity grew. I felt like I was on the verge of a revelation, one that would shake the very foundations of my understanding.

My journal entries chronicled my descent into madness. The words on the pages were the ramblings of a man who had lost his grip on reality. I wrote of tormenting visions, strange symbols etched in the snow, and an ever-present, pulsating force that guided my every move. The entity's whispers became my constant companions, urging me to venture deeper into the wilderness, to seek out the heart of darkness.

As time passed, I transformed into a mere shadow of my former self. Gaunt and wild-eyed, I was driven by an insatiable thirst for the entity's revelations. My journal became a testament to my descent into madness, filled with fragmented thoughts and paranoid rants.

I followed the entity's calls deeper and deeper into the wilderness, my grip on reality slipping away. I lost track of time, of the world outside. I became a slave to the entity's influence, a puppet dancing to its malevolent tune.

My journey ended in a cryptic and disjointed message, hinting at a revelation too immense to comprehend. The entity had ensnared me completely, leaving behind a legacy of dread in the icy expanse of the Alaskan wilderness.

As I look back on those fateful days in the Alaskan wilderness, there's a chilling realization that gnaws at the edges of my consciousness. The whispers in the wind, the haunting visions, and the relentless pursuit of that otherworldly presence – they all hint at an eerie connection, one I couldn't fully comprehend at the time.

It's as if I was drawn into a cosmic drama, a story far larger than the confines of my own existence. The entity's influence, the same one that guided me into madness, held a power that reached beyond the boundaries of the Alaskan wilderness.

I can't help but wonder if I was merely a pawn in a malevolent game, a player unwittingly chosen by forces I couldn't begin to understand. The strange symbols I encountered, the pulsating force that seemed to control my every move – they all hinted at a web of connections that stretched far beyond my own comprehension.

The question remains, how did I come into contact with this entity's influence? Was it mere chance, or was I chosen for a purpose that remains hidden in the shadowy depths of the cosmos? These are questions that haunt me, even now, as I grapple with the lingering dread of my past experiences.

As I reflect on those eerie days in the Alaskan wilderness, a profound sense of foreboding clings to my memories. The chilling events that transpired during my time there continue to haunt me, and I can't escape the feeling that my obsession with that otherworldly presence was no mere coincidence.

The cosmic horror that enveloped me hints at a reality far more unsettling than I ever imagined. It's a reminder that the entity's in-fluence, the same malevolent force that guided my actions, extends its dark tendrils to places one wouldn't expect. The Alaskan wilderness, a remote and desolate landscape, was just one of its many canvases.

As I write these words, I'm left to contemplate the implications of my own experiences and the ominous realization that the entity's reach knows no bounds. Was I chosen, or was I simply in the wrong place at the wrong time? The uncertainty lingers, and the cosmic horror that I faced in the wilderness continues to cast its shadow over my existence.

28

The Artic Researcher

I find myself in the unforgiving embrace of the Arctic, stationed in a remote outpost where the days are endless and the nights are filled with horrors beyond my wildest imagination. It started with vivid nightmares, relentless visions of ancient civilizations and their otherworldly rituals. The dreams are vivid, unsettling, and drenched in cosmic horror.

I can't escape the feeling that these nightmares are more than mere figments of my imagination. They seem to claw their way into my consciousness, each night more vivid and terrifying than the last. I witness eldritch ceremonies, unearthing forbidden knowledge that defies human understanding. The very fabric of reality itself seems to unravel in the presence of these cosmic horrors.

The toll these nightmares take on my mental and emotional well-being is immeasurable. I wake up each day with a sense of dread, the memories of those surreal, terrifying visions lingering like a curse. The lines between my waking life and the dreamworld blur, leaving me in a constant state of unease.

As I continue my research in this desolate place, I can't help but wonder if there's a deeper connection between these nightmares and the enigmatic entity we encountered. The chilling thought that the horrors I witness in my sleep might be tied to the malevolent force that haunts our Arctic outpost only deepens my distress.

My descent into madness is a relentless journey into the unknown, fueled by the unending nightmares that plague my nights. As the story unfolds, it becomes clear that the line between reality and illusion is blurring beyond recognition. The visions from my dreams have seeped into my waking life, casting a shadow over my every thought and action.

I find myself consumed by an all-encompassing obsession, an insatiable need to unearth the truth behind the ancient civilization and the presence that torments me in my dreams. My research notes have become a labyrinth of madness, filled with scribbles and incoherent ramblings as I try to piece together the fragments of knowledge I've gathered.

The weight of this relentless pursuit bears down on my deteriorating mental state. I can no longer distinguish between the waking world and the nightmarish landscapes I traverse in my sleep. Each day is a struggle to maintain a semblance of sanity as the nightmares bleed into my reality.

The nightmares have become my only reality, and I fear that they hold the key to understanding the malevolent force that has cast its shadow over our Arctic outpost. But as I delve deeper into this cosmic horror, I can't help but wonder if the price of this knowledge is my own descent into the abyss of madness.

As I venture further into the abyss of my own nightmares, I can't help but fixate on the unearthly presence that haunts my dreams. It's as if there's something beyond the veil of my subconscious, something ancient and powerful, reaching out to me through the twisted landscapes of my nightmares.

The questions gnaw at my sanity like a relentless hunger. What is this presence, and why has it chosen me as its vessel for communication? Is it a force of malevolence or something beyond human comprehension? My obsession with these questions only grows stronger with each passing day.

The atmosphere around me has become increasingly eerie and unsettling. The Arctic outpost, once a place of scientific inquiry and isolation, now feels like the epicenter of cosmic horrors. I find myself constantly on edge, my thoughts consumed by the unknown, and my dreams invaded by the eldritch visions that refuse to release their grip on my psyche.

The unearthly presence that I've come to believe is reaching out to me is a source of both dread and fascination. It's as if I've been chosen to be the conduit for something far beyond human understanding, and the weight of that revelation is both exhilarating and terrifying. My obsession with uncovering the truth intensifies, even as I fear the consequences of what I may ultimately discover.

29

The Seafarer's Log

I was part of a doomed Antarctic expedition, and my log entries tell a story of madness and despair. Each page is filled with cryptic symbols, unsettling drawings, and references to an enigmatic entity believed to be hidden beneath the ice.

As I transcribe my experiences, I can't help but feel a growing fixation on the entity. It's as if it has left an indelible mark on my very soul, and my thoughts are constantly consumed by the horrors I witnessed. The enigmatic symbols and drawings in my log entries represent a desperate attempt to make sense of the incomprehensible.

The narrative I've left behind is one of harrowing events and existential dread. I knew, even as I chronicled our descent into madness, that we were in the presence of a cosmic horror beyond human understanding. The very ice beneath our feet seemed to pulse with malevolence, and I couldn't escape the feeling that we were insignificant pawns in a cosmic game.

The log entries are a chilling testament to the horrors we faced, and they serve as a warning to any who would dare to venture into the heart of the Antarctic darkness. The entity that lurked beneath the ice is a force beyond reckoning, and its influence lingers in my nightmares, even as I pen these final words.

As I continue to transcribe these log entries, the depths of my paranoia become more evident. It's as if the entity's presence has seeped into my very being, and I can't help but feel that it played a malevolent role in the expedition's tragic fate.

My log entries reveal my increasing fear and suspicion of the entity. I'm convinced that it is somehow linked to the disaster that befell our ill-fated journey. The cryptic symbols and drawings that fill the pages are a reflection of my obsession with the enigmatic force that lurked beneath the ice.

The narrative I've left behind is a testament to my unraveling mind. I felt as though the entity's influence was inescapable, and I couldn't trust anyone, not even my fellow expedition members. Paranoia gnawed at my sanity, and I documented it all in the log, hoping to make sense of the senseless.

As I look back on those harrowing days, I can't help but wonder if we were mere playthings in a cosmic game. The entity's presence remains a haunting specter in my nightmares, and the paranoia it sowed continues to torment me, even as I inscribe these final words.

My every thought, my every waking moment, was consumed by the enigmatic entity that dwelled beneath the ice. As I transcribed my experiences into these log entries, it became increasingly apparent that my fixation on this malevolent force was the core of my narrative.

The log is a testament to my obsession with understanding and confronting the entity. Its cryptic symbols and haunting drawings serve as a constant reminder of the inexplicable horrors we faced during that cursed expedition. The more I recorded, the more I descended into an abyss of paranoia and fear.

I was convinced that the entity played a pivotal role in the expedition's catastrophic outcome, and my log entries were a desperate attempt to make sense of the unfathomable. The enigmatic presence continued to haunt me, even now, as I pen these final words. It is a fixation that has become an inescapable part of my existence, a darkness that refuses to release its hold on my soul.

30

The Lost Climber

My journey through the unforgiving peaks of Antarctica was nothing short of perilous. The biting cold and treacherous terrain seemed insurmountable, but an inexplicable force guided me relentlessly. It urged me forward, deeper into the icy heart of the wilderness.

The narrative of my experience was etched in the relentless snow and unforgiving winds that howled through the frozen expanse. The more I descended into the depths, the more I felt an eerie presence, an entity that seemed to beckon me toward a subterranean entrance hidden in the frigid landscape.

The story of my descent was one of growing dread, as I became entangled with the entity's influence. It was as if an invisible hand pushed me further into the abyss, compelling me to discover the secrets hidden beneath the ice. I couldn't escape the sensation that I was a pawn in a cosmic game, and the entity's influence was an inescapable part of my story.

My diary entries chronicled my descent into madness as I ventured further into the icy abyss. The frigid wasteland seemed to stretch endlessly before me, and the influence of the entity I encountered gnawed at my sanity.

I became convinced that this entity was no ordinary force; it was a cosmic power beyond human comprehension. My writings grew increasingly erratic as I grappled with the notion that I had stumbled upon something far greater than myself.

The narrative of my downward spiral was marked by a growing obsession to understand the entity and its cosmic significance. Each entry was a window into my deteriorating mental state, where the lines between reality and delusion blurred, and the entity's influence continued to tighten its grip on my psyche.

As I continued my perilous journey, I couldn't escape the overwhelming feeling that the entity guiding me had transcended the boundaries of human comprehension. My diary entries were filled with my fixation on understanding its purpose and nature, even as it inexorably urged me toward the subterranean entrance.

The words I wrote in my diary were infused with an atmosphere of existential horror. I grappled with a growing sense of dread, knowing that I had encountered something far greater and more terrible than myself. My conviction that this entity was a cosmic force beyond the limits of human understanding became an ever-present torment as I delved deeper into the frigid abyss.

31

The Deep-Sea Diver

As I descended into the frigid waters off Antarctica, my heart pounded with both excitement and trepidation. The underwater world held mysteries, and I was determined to explore them. The story of my chilling journey beneath the surface began with the discovery of an eerie underwater cave, a place untouched by human exploration. It was here that my unease began to take root.

My diary entries detailed the profound sense of unease that grew as I ventured deeper into the cave. The once crystal-clear waters seemed to darken and thicken as I delved further into the abyss, and I could feel the entity's influence all around me. The narrative captured my growing dread as I realized that I had stumbled upon something far more ominous and beyond my comprehension.

My journey into the icy depths beneath Antarctica was marked by my relentless pursuit of knowledge about the entity's ancient origins. The eerie underwater cave became a place of intrigue and terror, and my recordings and writings began to reflect my obsession with unraveling the truth.

As I ventured further into the abyss, the dark waters seemed to come alive with whispers and shadows. My diary entries and recordings detailed my determination to uncover the entity's past and the horrors that lurked below the surface. The narrative captured my growing fixation on the enigmatic force and the unyielding drive to reveal its secrets.

The terror below the surface of those frigid waters was palpable as I ventured deeper into the eerie underwater cave. My obsession with the entity's ancient origins grew, and a mounting dread accompanied my every move. It was as if the shadows of the deep were closing in around me, whispering secrets and ancient horrors that were awakening in the abyss.

My recordings and writings chronicled this descent into underwater terror, each entry reflecting my growing fixation on the entity and the fear that gnawed at me as I delved further into the depths. The narrative painted a vivid picture of a man haunted by what he was discovering below the surface, convinced that the entity was connected to something far more sinister and ancient than he could have ever imagined.

32

Afterword

by

Magnum Tenebrosum

As you turn the final pages of "Arctic Nightmare," I feel compelled to offer you a solemn warning, dear reader. While the horrors contained within these stories are, in many ways, the product of my own dark imagination, they also serve as a reflection of the very real fears that we must confront in our existence.

The entity, the obsession, the descent into madness—all are metaphors for the demons that can haunt us in our own lives. We live in a world that is far more complex and, at times, far more horrifying than we can ever hope to comprehend. The unknown is not limited to the pages of a book, but is a part of our daily reality.

It is essential to remember that our own obsessions, whether they be with power, knowledge, or something else entirely, can lead us down treacherous paths. The entity's influence is a symbol of the malevolent forces that can tempt us, and the descent into madness, a cautionary tale about the fragility of our own sanity.

As you ponder the cosmic horror themes that permeate these tales, I urge you to reflect on the real world, where the unknown lurks in the shadows. We must not be blind to the existential dread that comes with acknowledging our insignificance in the face of vast, incomprehensible forces.

In the spirit of Lovecraftian horror, "Arctic Nightmare" serves as a reminder that the true horrors often lie not in the supernatural, but in our own human nature and the mysteries of the universe. The un-known, the obsession, the descent into madness—they are all part of the intricate tapestry of our existence.

So, let these stories be a guide and a warning. As you close this book and return to the mundane world, remember that the horrors you've encountered are not confined to fiction. They are woven into the fabric of reality itself, and it is up to us to face them with courage and wisdom.

Magnum Tenebrosum

Milton Keynes UK
Ingram Content Group UK Ltd.
UKHW020926201123
432908UK00021B/3171